Print ISBN:

978-1-7780254-6-4

Editing by: Word Whisperer Literary Editing

Cover Design by: Whiskers & Whimsy Designs

Flame For You

RALEIGH DAMSON

CONTENTS

To my first readers... to readers who became friends... Blogland, this one goes
out to you.

1

CHAPTER ONE

Quinn Walsh circled the high-back chair, studying the pretty submissive who sat completely bound in rope. Here, backstage at Club Bandit, the private BDSM Club he'd been proud to be a founding member of, was the last place he thought he'd be tonight. Quinn smirked, knowing several members of the eager crowd would gladly trade places with him.

They were twenty minutes behind schedule. He could hear the eagerness ripple through the crowd. The low base of the techno music pumping out of the speakers fuelled the anticipation, but Quinn would not rush, despite the waiting audience.

He checked the knots, pulling on sections of the soft red rope. Technically, he couldn't find fault. Logan Marrock, his friend and experienced rigger, had tied it. He had to give his friends credit; they upped their game. Over the last few months, he'd ignored their calls. But when Logan had texted tonight, asking for help with this extreme rope suspension, he couldn't say no to a Bandit Brother. Even if the timing sucked.

"Come on! We've practiced this, and the carabiners will take the weight. She'll fly up nice and easy."

"You have no fear of this?" he asked Clara, the submissive in the chair.

"Quinn, she has the experience. Let's get on with it."

"You called me for an opinion and a second look." Quinn glared at his friend. "I'm asking Clara. How is your circulation?"

The petite woman wiggled her fingers, and he checked the slack on the rope. He glanced above him at the metal pulley system. The steel hooks lowered from the thick cable wires hanging from the stage lighting poles above.

"I trust the physics. We tested it with sandbags, and the spiderweb of ropes on the legs helped to distribute the weight." Logan tugged on the wire cables hooked to the top of the chair.

Quinn grunted.

"I didn't make her sign an extra waiver," Zee Ridell, the grey-haired, goateed owner of Club Bandit, came out from the wings, wearing a headset, and clapped Quinn on the back.

"Untie the chest harness and re-tie it so it's not wrapped around the chair." Quinn pointed at the rope crisscrossing over Clara's chest and then bound to the chair.

"Yeah, I can see your reasoning." Logan started untying the length of rope across Clara's chest and from the chair. If he needed further proof that this wasn't the place for him, seeing Logan re-tie a chest harness did nothing. He admired his friend's skill, but he didn't wish he was the one tying.

In the end, the effect looked just as badass. With Clara's breasts standing up for attention, her creamy skin glowed against the red rope. The knots on her legs and wrists secured her, and she looked like the perfect, willing captive. Quinn felt as confident as he could that no harm would come from this stunt.

His friends trusted his judgment. Assessing risks was what he did—or what he'd used to do. He couldn't do it anymore, not after the clusterfuck on the last job.

"You're not a novice. You've belayed for me lots of times. This is no different." Logan's gift for reading the room extended to reading his mind.

Logan's right, but his analytical mind kept running through the possibilities. The pulley system they made could more than handle this job. He knew Logan and Zee had run through this suspension multiple times, but he didn't trust his gut. Not anymore, not after that one day in June.

"You can do this." Logan crouched down in front of the submissive, kissed her on the forehead. Quinn swallowed a lump in his throat. He found the intimacy displayed in BDSM sexy as hell and maybe he missed it—a smidge.

"I'm ready!" Clara's cheeks flushed with excitement.

"Here, you do the honours." Logan handed him a cell phone. "Click the icons on the app to change the speed of the vibrator. She's not coming down until she screams."

"This isn't enough to keep me here, you know." But he took the phone. Whatever, it would get him out of here faster. His friend knew Quinn loved making subs lose their guarded control. And Logan loved spectacles, taking something intimate and making a performance out of it, and it was interesting to watch, but the type of submission Quinn lived for was the kind wrought by an audience of one.

"I need you for three minutes or three hours. What do you think, little sub? How long is it going to take you to come in front of all those people, up in the air like that?" the sub closed her eyes under Logan's touch. Quinn couldn't help but smile, knowing Clara was wearing the vibrator under her black lacey panties.

"Not long," Clara murmured.

"We'll find out." Logan clapped his hands together.

"Telling them to open curtains," Zee spoke into the headset.

"Here we go," Logan signalled a countdown of five.

The curtain parted, the gasps and exclamations rolled through the crowd. Quinn's shoulders tightened, and he ground his molars. But he zeroed in and fell back on his experience, his hands sure on the smooth rope.

"Now, for my first and only trick of the evening, I will raise this submissive to the rafters!" Logan flashed a grin at the audience "With the help of my gorgeous assistant, Quinn."

Quinn gave him the finger. The crowd laughed.

"Let's raise this submissive to the rafters!"

At each pull of the rope, the chair lifted higher. The crowd cheered.

Quinn trampled down his impatience. Leaving in the middle of a suspension would be bad form, but he considered it for a moment.

Logan waved at the crowd, encouraging their applause. One last dramatic pull brought the chair inches from the ceiling.

"How's the view from there, Clara?"

"Awesome," Clara said.

"Should we leave you hanging out there all night?"

"I think your arms will be tired before mine," Logan said.

Quinn felt his lips twitch, and the audience laughed.

"Want to try me?" Logan's voice lowered.

Quinn snorted.

"No, Sir."

"Only one way I'm going to let you down. Do you remember?"

Clara smiled. "Yes, Sir."

Quinn took that as his cue, taking the rope in one hand and tapping the "pulse" icon on his phone with his other.

A slight shiver made Clara shift in her seat. "When I have an orgasm, you'll let me down."

"Yes. Do you think you can come with all these people watching you?" the crowd loved this, and someone sent out a sharp whistle.

"Yes, Sir," Clara said with a breathy voice, struggling against the ropes as the vibrator pulsed against her needy, exposed clit.

Quinn pressed the "vibrate" icon on the app, and Clara closed her eyes as the sensations changed.

"All these people watching you, hanging here tied up in a chair. How is it making you feel?" Logan's low voice carried with the resonance of a dominant in total control.

"Exposed," Clara whispered as she tried to thrust against the red ropes that bound her in place.

"Turned on?" Quinn couldn't help but ask. He wanted to strangle Logan. He hadn't counted on being in a scene.

"So turned on!"

"Good. Let's see if you'll scream above all these people. Rack it up, Quinn."

"My pleasure." Quinn pressed the icon for "bounce." He couldn't help the thrill that travelled through his body at the sight of Clara, tied on the chair, the charge of being connected to her through the rope in his hand, and the control of the vibrator in the other.

"That should do it. Let go, Clara." Damn, he missed being in charge of a woman's orgasm.

"I see you, Clara. You're beautiful, tied up in my ropes, suspended above all these people. Come for us, darling." Logan pulled on the ropes, causing the chair to sway.

When Quinn saw her face scrunch up, her hands grip the arms of the chair; he changed the intensity of the vibrations coursing through her again, pressing the icon for "peak."

Clara's mouth opened in a wide O, and for a second, she slumped forward.

"Looks like you came, my sweet rope bunny. Enough to let you down, do you think? What happened to that scream?"

Clara shook with laughter, the stage lights picking up the streak of tears rolling down her face.

"Yes, please," Clara whispered. "I couldn't scream."

"What do you think, everyone?" Logan turned to the crowd.

Gentle clapping rolled through the crowd.

"You gave us a show, Clara," Logan beamed, his voice thick with praise.

"We're going to bring you down, nice and slow now," Quinn said, sliding the phone in his pocket and taking the ropes in both hands.

Bringing his left hand under his right, Quinn steadied the rope. On Logan's signal, he let the rope feed through the belay device, keeping a pace that matched Logan's on the opposite side, so the chair didn't tip.

A slow and steady half-minute later, the chair and Clara landed on the black stage floor, and the crowd applauded.

"Next time, we should do two chairs," Logan grinned. He rushed over to Clara, caressed her shoulders, and kissed her cheek. "Good girl, I'll untie these ropes."

"Delighted to lend a hand. Going now." He gave Logan his phone back and took advantage of him being occupied, but Quinn didn't want another argument about why he should stay in town.

The red textured walls and shining hardwood floors lent the cavernous space a warm and luxurious air. Soft lighting highlighted various play stations scattered around the perimeter of the room.

Quinn moved through the crowd, shrugging off attempts at small talk from the other members. Not that long ago, Club Bandit felt like a second home, and even though he thought Club Bandit and Bandit Brothers silly names, he was damn grateful for both.

The soothing space couldn't calm Quinn's angst, and he rushed for the exit.

Here in this place, with lashes of leather in the background, the cries of passion, it contained too much life. And he couldn't escape the fact that he felt half-dead inside. The thick air of excitement made his chest tight. Almost like he couldn't breathe. He wanted an escape.

His brother Jordan coined the five of them "Bandit Brothers" from their army days, and the name expanded, encompassing their small, tight-knit group of private operatives who worked for Axis Management after they finished with the military. The five of them were members of Team Stealth, security operatives whose primary job consisted of going in and getting out with no one knowing they were ever there.

Club Bandit took inspiration from the name when Zee converted the old staff quarters of his mansion into a BDSM Club. He joked he couldn't be in their club, so he had to create one of his own. Six months ago, Quinn would have been whipping his then-sub, Rachel, right next to his buddy and fellow Bandit Brother, Nick Laurent, but things changed.

Like when Rachel screamed at him to whip her harder and Quinn refused, she said, "You're not man enough to hit me." Quinn dismissed her right then and there because he hated manipulation. He should have cut ties earlier for the way Rachel had treated his sister. He should have done it because no matter what he'd given Rachel, it was never enough.

"Not feeling it?" Gabe Arthur, another Bandit Brother asked him, walking alongside him. His eyes fell on X cross in the corner, and a wave of grief hit Quinn in the centre of his chest. It was his fault he didn't have anyone.

"I'm leaving." His phone vibrated in his pocket.

"You can be a part of it, Quinn. You don't have to go," Gabe said.

With his heart thundering in his chest, Quinn kept walking.

He refused to let go of the potent mix of grief and pain. Instead, he cocooned himself in it, cutting himself off from his friends and family. If he let the reins holding his pain go, it would take him under.

"Quinn." Logan's firm hand on his shoulder stopped him in his stride. "Call me when you're home."

"I don't need another mother." Quinn shook off Logan's arm.

His friend put his hands up in a placating gesture.

Quinn sighed. He'd put Logan through hell these last few months, and his friend didn't deserve him being an asshole now.

Quinn extended his fist, and Logan bumped it back.

Quinn started to turn to the exit but stopped. "What the fuck?" He growled out the words.

"He's our brother." Logan's hand came around Quinn's arm.

Quinn glared at the brick wall of a man standing in front of him. *Erik fucking Knight.* The bastard he'd never wanted to see again.

Quinn would always blame himself, but the man in front of him didn't do his job. In the night's dark, from the depths of his self-pity, Quinn often turned it over in his head, asking himself whose fault it was that Jordan was dead. His or Erik's? The answer depended on the night.

"He's not my brother."

Erik passed Quinn and disappeared into the door on the left, marked 'Private.'

Quinn breathed through his nose, barely managing not to slam the club's door behind him. He marched over to his truck and fought for self-control, this time resisting the urge to pound his fist into metal.

Getting in his truck, he grabbed his phone from the console, seeing his sister's number. Listening to the message, Quinn cursed.

He wasn't going anywhere tonight.

2

CHAPTER TWO

The restaurant off the highway didn't look like it had a paint job in fifty years. Every tile on the black-and-white floor cracked. Ripped faux leather on the booths, and the lighting fixtures belonged in an antique shop, yet the place sparkled.

Typical for Kayleigh, she hadn't arrived. Quinn signalled for coffee. A total bastard move, not telling his little sister he was leaving town. Quinn dragged a hand over his scruffy face. His sister's message said she needed to talk and gave the address of this restaurant to meet. With Kayleigh, "talk" could mean anything from sobbing over a break-up to sharing a new promotion, to being upset that the woman at the nail salon didn't do a good job.

"Here's your coffee." The server placed the steaming mug in front of him.

Quinn gave the older woman a nod. "Thanks."

The chime above the door sounded, and he glanced up.

Not his sister. A thin man with long shaggy yellow hair, dressed in an oversized coat and sunglasses, stopped beside his table.

"You need money?" Quinn asked the guy.

"You the fire guy?" he asked.

The man swayed back and forth. A discreet sniff didn't reveal any alcohol smell. The man kept looking around, hopping on his feet.

Quinn played along for now. "Sure. I'm the fire guy."

The man opened his jacket, stuck his arm in the deep pocket, and threw a manila envelope on the table.

"Fifty thousand up front, as we agreed, and fifty thousand when complete. You have seventy-two hours to make sure the chick is inside the house."

Man, this guy had to be high on something. "Are you sure you're okay?"

"Shush," the man shook his head frantically, held his finger to his lips. "Can I trust you or not?"

"I'm an old pro. You can trust me." Quinn nodded. Experience had taught him it was better to play along.

"Give me an email." The guy held out his phone.

"All right, just a minute here." He created a dummy email and plugged it into the guy's phone.

The guy tapped at his screen, giving Quinn a thumbs-up. "You should have the transfer in half an hour."

"Got it," Quinn tapped his screen.

The man rapped his hand on the table, spun around, and left.

Quinn strode to the window, observing the man as he swayed on his feet for a moment, then he zigzagged toward the highway

An alert chimed on his phone, fifty thousand dollars waiting to be deposited at the bank of his choice. Quinn let out a low whistle.

He finished his coffee, opened a menu, and planned to stick around to see if his sister and the "fire guy," the guy planned on meeting, showed. He ran his hands over the envelope, finding nothing solid.

Quinn jabbed at his phone, sending a text.

"What will you have, sugar?"

"Your burgers are fresh?"

"Sure are."

"I'll take one with a side of fries and an iced tea."

"You got it."

Quinn slid open the envelope, and a glossy 8X10 headshot fell out.

He'd never believed his mother's insistence that people could feel from looking at an image... But the simple photo set off an explosion inside his otherwise empty shell of a body—a firestorm of need.

This picture of a honey blond beauty with brown eyes flecked with gold caused his dormant libido to flare to life. Less than an hour ago, he'd stood in a BDSM club full of naked women. He'd spent the first half of the evening turning down alluring invitations because his head wasn't in the right place. Staring at this photo cut through his grief sandstorm. He imagined kissing those berry pink lips, running his hands through that honey hair, and wondering what sounds he could coax from that pretty mouth.

He read the name scrawled at the bottom in sharpie.

"Let's see who you are, Simone Roberts." He entered her name on his phone and cursed as the results flooded his screen. Simone Roberts was an interior designer, a local celebrity, with a DIY Design segment on the morning show.

Quinn wondered if she had any media training at all and decided not based on her random posts. Someone planned to kill her, and she posted her life online. If Quinn had his way with her, he would spank her ass red for being so careless.

For now, he could take advantage of her lack of filter. She'd told him and the world exactly where she would be tomorrow night.

His past life in the army, with a stint in CSIS, gave him skills. He might not be fit to run another op for Axis Management, but he could keep this woman safe.

He dialled a buddy at the police department.

On this long weekend, no one rushed to the phone. Giving that up, he tried Ares Montague, co-owner of Axis Management, his sometimes boss and friend. No luck.

The server set down the grub, and Quinn ate as he watched people come in and out, nobody looked as if they were an arsonist waiting around. Damn if it wasn't one of the best burgers he ever ate.

He wiped his mouth and hands with a napkin, took a long pull on his iced tea, and ordered another coffee. He texted Kayleigh, asking for her ETA, and received no answer, which didn't surprise him. Kayleigh could be flighty. It wouldn't surprise him if she'd changed her mind.

After another half hour, Quinn paid his bill, adding a twenty for a tip. He left a message, for the other Montague brother, Xander, telling him he needed a place to crash and climbed into his truck, throwing the envelope with Simone's headshot on the passenger seat.

Hell, he had no business getting involved here, but his mind kicked into high gear, making a list of what he had to do, who he would call. He couldn't ignore those berry pink lips or the golden hair that framed an oval face, posed with a half-smile.

He must find this woman. She was unaware of the danger. If the threat to her was real, and the transfer of money gave him the evidence to make him believe it was, he needed to act fast. The criminal who'd hired him might have a backup plan.

3

CHAPTER THREE

"Hey, sorry to interrupt, but are you, Simone Roberts, from the morning show?"

The point-and-shoot camera slipped from her fingers and clinked against the white ceramic vase of white hydrangeas. Simone had been so focused on taking a perfectly balanced photo of the centrepiece, she hadn't heard the man come up behind her. She didn't enjoy talking with strangers but smiled at the large, grey-bearded man.

"Yes, I have the DIY Design segment." She tucked a piece of stray hair behind her ear and picked up the camera.

"My wife loves you. She's at me to put hooks up in the front closet," the man said.

"Paul, come dance with me!" a woman called over from the next table.

"Come on over here, Rita! This is Simone Roberts I'm talking to." Paul grinned. His wife stepped beside him, a furious blush spreading over her face.

"Oh! I just love your show. You're the best-dressed bridesmaid too! Your hair is so pretty. You look shorter in real life than on TV. Can I get your autograph?"

"Rita, leave her alone," Paul said.

Simone bit her lip, trying not to laugh. If Paul wanted her left alone, he shouldn't have pulled his wife over. In the eight months she'd had the show, she still wasn't used to people stopping her. When they did, she felt nervous and out of sorts, unsure what to do or say, but the more people she met, the more practiced she got at it and realized they were just as nervous with her.

"Here." Simone reached for a pen and scribbled her name on the back of a table seating name tag. "Nice to meet you, Rita and Paul."

"Thank you!" Rita gushed.

Simone returned her wave and moved to the next silk-covered table, under the golden fairy lights of the white organza draped ballroom.

Smiling at guests, she excused herself as she reached over their empty coffee cups, intent on capturing each detail. The bride, Meredith Phillips, had made sure every guest had a point and shoot camera, and she wanted them put to use. From the close-up of the way the white and gold round hanging lanterns cast their glow on the white embroidered linen napkins to the overflowing dessert table, Simone wanted her best friend to have all the details of this day captured forever. Standing in the centre of the vast ballroom, she pointed and clicked at the head table high on a platform at the front of the ballroom. Simone frowned and considered deleting it. Her best friend Ava, sister of the bride, sat slumped in her golden-covered chair, passing a half-full shot glass back and forth between her hands.

"Simone, want to dance?"

She looked up at Owen, the tall, lanky groomsman, her partner for the wedding, and heat rushed to her face. The dance floor at this reception resembled a club, a favourite design choice of Simone's. Glancing at Ava, she shook her head. She had to keep her friend from getting smashed.

"Maybe the next one?" She bit her lip and shrugged, apologetically.

"Sure." Owen nodded and grabbed a Happy Ever After off the tray of a passing server. He sipped the cocktail Ava, Simone, and Meredith had created for today and winced. "I thought you guys chugged these because they tasted good." He put the martini glass down on a nearby table.

"It's an acquired taste, plus it's pink." Simone laughed.

Mielle, another bridesmaid came dancing over, she grabbed Owen's hands and pulled him towards the dance floor. Come on, Owen!"

Simone gave them a wave and walked up to the platform, sitting down in her chair next to Ava. She took off her shoes and rubbed her aching feet.

"The reception looks great, doesn't it?"

"Exactly how the bride wanted it," Ava said, her arms crossed in front of her.

White sparkly drapery covered the ballroom from floor to ceiling. The lone section not covered in white was the view of the mountains from out the window, with the lights from the city twinkling below. The hanging white drapery in the ceiling took on yellow and green hues as the flashing lights from the sunken dance floor lit it up with the change of the beat. Simone swayed in her chair and grinned when her gaze landed on Meredith in her red and gold brocade wedding gown in the arms of her new husband, Jeffery.

"Are you sure you need another one?" Simone asked as Ava gestured at the server for another drink.

"Yeah, I do." Ava spun her empty glass. "All of it comes so easy for her." She flipped her long black braid off her shoulder.

"Your sister has the luck to go along with her talent." Simone knew that got to Ava occasionally.

"Yep, she got everything she wanted right away." The snarky tone of Ava's voice caught Simone off guard.

Simone loved seeing Meredith happy. She deserved a happily ever after. Her caring friend never let the success of her television show go to her head. Simone smiled, remembering how she had met Meredith. They'd both just started at university, and Meredith was running late for an audition. She'd stood digging through her purse for lipstick in the library's lobby while waiting for a cab when Simone proffered her rose-hued lipstick and offered to drive her to the audition.

They'd hit it off immediately. Meredith texted her the next, thanking her for the ride and letting Simone know she'd landed the part she had auditioned for, the lead on a crime drama that skyrocketed her acting career.

The next weekend, Meredith invited Simone to her house for the first Create-a-Cocktail session, introducing her to her younger sister. The three women became close friends and Simone was grateful for them. Without Ava and Meredith, she wasn't sure she could have survived the last six months.

"You had it easy, too. You didn't even have to audition for your show," Ava said.

Simone's face grew hot. Her ex-mother-in-law, Marion, had told her the breakfast show had a space to fill. Simone said she would be interested, and after one meeting with the production team, she was in.

"Ava, you're a talented make-up artist. You'll get your break. How is working at the comedy club?"

"Not exactly what I want," Ava said. "But more people see the make-up I do through the comedy club's social media. I'm just tired."

Simone smiled. Her friend had moonlighted at the comedy club for over a year, and she'd seemed tired through this week of wedding preparations.

Ava grabbed a Happy Ever After cocktail from the server's tray.

"Yeah, it has been a long day." Simone sipped her cocktail.

"I shouldn't be whining to you." Ava lifted her head from her arm, knocked back the Happy Ever After in one gulp. "This whole thing must have been horrible for you. Kind of insensitive of Meredith to ask you to be a bridesmaid. That's like drinking the crappy vodka because it's all you got, right?" Ava giggled.

"Ava!" Simone playfully slapped her friend's arm. On the dance floor, the newlyweds locked lips, and a twinge of envy stirred in the pit of her stomach. "No. I'm thrilled Meredith asked me." Simone smiled. "Some excitement to brighten up my boring life."

Even though helping Meredith pick out bridesmaid dresses and choosing decorations had tugged at her wounded heart, Simone felt honoured to be a part of her friend's wedding.

"You had a boring life with Liam," Ava said.

"It wasn't terrible," Simone said.

"The sock drawer..." Ava pointed a long, slender, manicured, gel-tipped finger at Simone. "...that isn't filled with socks."

Simone shook her head, regretting telling Ava about her sock drawer filled with lost opportunities and hopes. From their first Christmas, the vouchers to take dance lessons at a studio, then the tickets to learn to fly an airplane that she had given Liam for his birthday, and from their second anniversary, the couple's massage and spa voucher she had purchased; all sat hidden and unused. Simone blushed, thinking about the contents of the drawer that she *hadn't* shared with Ava.

"This isn't what I imagined." Simone rubbed her empty ring finger. She knew ending her marriage to Liam had been the right thing to do, but she thought she would be married until she was old and grey.

But it didn't mean she wanted to open a dating profile or be set up on a date with any of their friends.

"Come on, you guys! One last round of photos!" Meredith came up to the table, reached over the tablecloth, and grabbed their hands.

"Okay, we're coming." Simone laughed and pulled Ava out of her chair.

"Almost over, right?" Ava grinned and leaned on Simone as they made their way to the photographer at the side of the ballroom.

"That's the spirit." Simone put her arm around her friend, and they joined the other wedding party members on the platform, flanking Meredith and Jeffery.

"Two more!" the photographer called.

As she posed for a photo in between Meredith and Ava, Simone squeezed her hands. Meredith's contagious joy made Simone's cheeks hurt from all her smiling. "Thank you so much for everything!" Meredith hugged her.

Simone kissed her on the cheek. "You're welcome. You're beautiful, and it was an exceptional wedding."

"I need another drink." Ava leaned on Simone for balance. "I don't get a thank you?" Meredith rolled her eyes. "Thank you, Ava, for showing up."

Meredith's husband whisked her away to the dance floor as guests clapped.

Steadying Ava, Simone got them over to the sleek, black chrome bar without falling over.

"Everyone loves her so much." Ava gestured with her filled pink martini glass.

Simone's heart twisted to see their father embrace Meredith. She remembered how happy her dad was on her wedding day. Her father had asked for so little from her, and she couldn't stay married. Her father was the reason she'd agreed to marry Liam.

"A smoking hot guy is checking you out, over by the wall." Ava slurred her words and pointed.

"What guy?" Simone asked. "He's checking you out."

She couldn't see around the tall bodies in front of the bar, but Ava was the one who always drew the attention of men, not her.

"Nope. That sex god's eyes are on you. He's coming this way." Ava giggled, leaning against her again. "Simone, I double dare you to dance with him. Better yet, as hot as he is, I dare you to bang him."

"Ava!" Simone swatted her friend's hand playfully. "I think I've forgotten how." Both of them collapsed into giggles.

"Go dance with him." Ava gave her a little push.

Simone shook her head but was happy to have Ava back to being herself.

Ava always egged her on to get out of her comfort zone.

"May I have the next dance?"

The deep, sultry voice sent a shiver down her spine. Simone turned around to find one giant, gorgeous man standing next to her. As his icy blue stare combed over her, butterflies flared to life in her stomach. Her heart pounded against her ribs.

He raised an eyebrow, extending his hand to her.

"Double dare," Ava whispered.

"I don't know." Those butterflies now twisted in knots as she wiped her palms against her gold bridesmaid gown. "I'm probably not your type."

"It's only a dance." The corners of his mouth turned up, and he raised an eyebrow, those magnificent blues laser-focused on her.

The reception was almost over, and she loved being on the dance floor. What did this guy want with her? Glancing at the stranger, she drank him in. His dark blue shirt perfectly pressed, his suit dark grey jacket fit over his muscled shoulders just right, and he stood there, patiently waiting for her to say something.

"Okay. One dance," Simone said.

She placed her hand in his outstretched one and, as his lips turned up in a smile, a thrill raced through her. He led them over to the dance floor. Even in the flashing neon lights, the man looked good.

When he twirled her away from him, she felt the strength of his forearm. He would have no trouble picking her up and throwing her around.

His hand came around the small of her back, holding her in place. "I'm sure you danced with a lot of partners before I got here."

Her face hot, Simone shook her head. "My bridesmaid duties kept me busy."

That dance ended and a slower, softer beat came on.

The man pulled her so close to his chest Simone could smell the woodsy cedar scent of his aftershave. She was sure he could hear her frantic heartbeat.

"What do you think my type is?" The corners of his mouth turned up.

Simone blushed.

"I don't know why I said that." Simone turned her head away.

"You must have a reason." He put a finger on her chin, bringing her head back to face him, and he stared at her so intently she couldn't look away.

"Men don't ask me to dance often. Not men like you." Simone said. God, maybe she had too much to drink.

"I feel judged," he said, smiling down at her.

"No, I didn't mean... I'm nervous," Simone stammered and wondered if she should just end the dance.

His hand brushed her cheek, his warmth spread through her, making her flushed and giddy. "Are you okay with this?" he asked her.

"Yes, it's fine." She put her hands on his shoulders, those butterflies jumping around to her erratic heartbeat.

"So, what did you think of the wedding?" He brought her close together, his hips pressed against her.

Heat flooded her cheeks. Her body felt feverish, and it took Simone a moment to recognize the ping of sensations as desire.

"Beautiful, the bride's dream come true," Simone grinned.

"Think they'll last?" the man whispered into her ear.

"You never know. I hope so," Simone said. "What about you?"

"I only bet on what I know for sure." His hands slid over her waist. Simone felt a flush creep up her neck.

"What's for sure?" She smiled at him, her fingertips feeling his muscled shoulders.

"That I'm dancing with the prettiest woman in the room." His hands moved in gentle circles, against her back His light touch felt good and it soothed Simone's nerves.

"You have some excellent lines." Simone ducked her head.

"And the moves to go with them." As the tempo changed, he brought her close to him, he, pressed his hips against hers.

"You like to be in control."

"I do."

His shocking blue eyes found and zeroed into her. Simone squirmed as heat from her centre flamed up to her face.

She wanted to touch his dark hair, which fell just above his eyebrows.

He grinned, the smile making his features softer, and placed his hands on her shoulders, bringing her against his hard plane of muscled chest.

"On the dance floor and in bed," he added, his breath tickling her ear.

Simone swallowed as he brought her closer, his firm hand on the small of her back.

"My type," he whispered into her ear, "is a woman who is honest with herself, a woman who knows what she wants. Do you know what you want?"

Of their own accord, her hands slid up his biceps. His words made her squirm. She took her hands off his arms, unsure what to do with them. "I don't know."

Her thoughts went blank, and her throat went dry.

He laughed and covered her hands with his and brought her hands on his waist. "You can touch me anywhere... I only bite when you ask for it," his tone dropped to a sultry vibration. Simone smiled, ducking her head. The heat of his body, the sultry way he looked at her, sent her pulse racing.

Fantasies of being dominated in the bedroom danced through her mind. One Valentine's Day, on a whim, she'd bought a flogger. The flogger had ended up in the sock drawer.

Whenever Simone brought up being kinky in the bedroom, her ex-husband has called her perverted.

"What's wrong?" the stranger asked her.

Simone shook off the memory of rejection and smiled. The man had made a joke, and she'd leapt to conclusions.

The music changed to a faster tempo, but instead of flinging her away from him he brought her closer, he rocked his hips against her again. Simone's throat went dry.

"That dress matches your hair," he said.

"What, this old thing?" Simone took off one of her hands from under his and ran it along her silky golden gown. The man smiled at her and put her hand back, and sparks flew through her body.

Her fluttering stomach stole the breath out of her, and as she met his, Simone blushed.

"I don't usually do this," she said as the music ended.

"Talk or dance?" the man asked.

"Dance."

"Then I hope you're enjoying this one," he said as the music changed. This time he flung her away, and Simone laughed, then he spun her back against his smooth wall of muscles.

4

CHAPTER FOUR

The music pulsed beneath her feet, and his firm grip pushed her away before spinning her back into his hard chest. His hands guided her to match steps and heat—not that from the hundreds of guests or the room—spread over her as she relaxed against him. This man's power and the intensity of his interest eased her loneliness and replaced it with adrenaline. His touch forced her out of her comfort zone, and Simone liked it.

"It's not every day your friend gets married." His hands slid down to her waist.

"It's not every day I dance with a hot stranger." She hadn't meant to say that and wished the floor would swallow her up.

"You think I'm hot?" he asked in a whisper.

Her pulse raced. She giggled nervously.

The MC announced the last call, and the music changed to a slower song.

"Want that drink?" he asked, offering her his arm.

"Yes." Wrapping her fingers around his arm made her feel daring, and he guided them through the crowd to the bar.

"What do you drink?"

"White wine, please."

"Quinn." He extended his hand.

Smiling, she grasped his hand. "Simone." His grip felt firm, holding onto the connection for a moment before letting go.

"Have I seen you around before?"

"Bridesmaid," she said, gesturing at her gold sheath. "You saw me at the ceremony, however many hours ago that was."

"I feel I've seen you somewhere else...before. Don't you have a TV show or something?"

His eyes held her gaze. She thought of one of her clients, who loved everything blue and wished she could get his shade of iris colour in paint.

"It's just a small half-hour segment," Simone mumbled.

"It may be half an hour, but your face is memorable," Quinn said.

One of those faces splayed on a billboard of the television station downtown and hard to miss in the midday traffic.

"Are you from Vancouver?" Quinn asked.

"Born and raised. You?"

"Not so lucky. I'm from a mining town in Northern Ontario. The winter starts in October."

"What brought you out here?" Simone asked.

"The excitement of the ocean and the mountains. And it doesn't drop to forty below in the winter."

Simone laughed, sipped her wine. "Have any siblings?"

"A younger sister," Quinn said. "You?"

Shaking her head, Simone set her wineglass down on the bar. "I'm an only child."

"Spoiled with involved parents?" Quinn's sensuous lips twitched.

"My parents doted on me, yes. How did you guess?" Simone's fingers brushed against his. A twinge of electricity made her mouth dry.

"Just a hunch." His mouth did that upturn thing again.

"Why don't we have another drink at my place? I have a well-stocked bar and a million-dollar view."

His fingers closed around hers and her pulse raced. She fidgeted with her wine glass under Quinn's gaze.

If I say yes, will he think I'm a slut? Simone bit her lip, wondering what it would be like to walk out of here with this chiselled and muscled stranger.

"I've been looking at a million-dollar view all night." Simone gestured at the wide, expansive windows that faced the mountains.

"My view is more private. What do you say?"

An electric flare of desire ran through her as Quinn slid off the barstool, crowding her space.

"This is like a fantasy." She couldn't meet his eyes. What a cheesy thing to say.

"What kind of fantasy?" he whispered into her ear.

Her insides formed a hard ball of nerves as Quinn's fingers grabbed her chin and lifted her head to meet his eyes.

Warmth licked at her cheeks as she looked at him. He hadn't moved. His hand was still on her arm.

"Hot guy sweeps me off the dance floor and into bed, fulfilling all my secret fantasies."

He leaned further into her space, his fingers walking up to her arm until he gently turned her around to face him, and the heat in her core sparked to life.

"What secret fantasies would those be?"

Her mouth went dry at his words, at the intensity of his gaze. He stood right beside her, a wall of muscle and warmth, a predatory look in those gemstone eyes.

"Quinn, I don't know you. You tell first."

Fascinating, how his laugh relaxed his features. Simone wanted to see him laugh again. Slowly, he glided his thumb over her knuckles. At his soft touch, the ball of tension in her unfurled.

"Hot girl I met at the wedding goes home with me," he said, his fiery gaze steady on her. "I tie her up and bring her to climax over and over again."

Deep in her stomach, a flare of excitement and shame went through her. Simone hid her flaming face by looking past Quinn at the dance floor. *Maybe he does this all the time.* She'd never had sex with a stranger. It had been a long time since a man tried to pick her up at the bar, and never mind the kinky stuff.

She laughed, and as she turned to look at the dance floor, she brushed against his arm.

"Tell me one fantasy." His voice dropped to a deeper octave, a tone of command. A slight tremble went through her fingers. He took her hand in his confident touch. A hot flush crept up her neck, but his steady gaze stilled her nerves.

"I've always wanted to be tied up." As soon as the words came out, she wished she could take them back. Simone stared at the floor as the fire in her cheeks rose to searing levels.

Quinn slung an arm around her. "You're speaking my language."

He even looked like a character from one of those steamy romance books. She liked his arm being around her, shielding her, as she disappeared in his height and width.

"I've never gone home with a stranger before," she whispered. Twinges of excitement danced along her nerve endings.

Quinn ran his knuckles down the side of her face. "I'm happy to be your first."

Simone shuddered. He leaned towards her, his mouth inches from hers. A flash of heat rose from her core. How would his lips feel against hers?

She shook her head, remembering Ava.

"I promised to stay until the end to look after my friend."

"I'm not going anywhere." He pulled her against him.

The music changed to an upbeat dance song, and family and friends clapped and cheered, forming a line for the newlyweds to walk through.

"Looks like the bride and groom are on their way out," Simone said.

"Let's go say goodbye." He extended his arm to her. Simone put her fingers around his muscled arm and let him weave them through the crowd to the front of the line.

"Simone!" Meredith cried.

Meredith ran over to them with her new husband in tow.

"You have the best time." Simone embraced her friend and focused on Jeffery. "You take care of her.

"I promised I would," Jeffery replied, smiling. Even his white teeth against his black beard seemed to sparkle with happiness.

"I love you!" Simone shouted.

Jeffery scooped his giggling bride in his arms, and the guests followed them to the elevator, clapping and cheering.

"Let's go, bride!"

Meredith blew kisses to them all until the doors swished closed.

"How about I whisk you away now?" Quinn's fingers ran along her collarbone. She lifted her head and stared into his blue eyes. Taking in his carved jawline and the well-defined Cupid's bow above his exquisite lips, Simone leaned towards him. His hand slid against her back, bringing her closer to his chest. Quinn leaned down, and Simone's breath hitched in her throat.

From behind them, a tremendous crash rang out. In the next minute, Simone found herself under his muscular body.

"Are you okay?" Quinn asked.

"I'm fine. I think my drunk friend knocked something over." Simone turned her head to see what caused the crash. "Military?"

"Army. How did you guess?"

Laughing, Simone reached up and touched his hair. "I saw it in a movie once."

"This is not how I want you under me." His sultry tone turned her insides to liquid.

Simone bit her lip, knowing her cheeks were flaming red.

She admired how gracefully he moved, lifting himself off the floor, using his powerful forearms while struggling to her feet.

"Thanks," she said as he helped her off the floor. "I've got to go check on Ava."

Simone bit her lip from laughing. Her friend sat in a puddle of water, roses, and hydrangeas, the broken vase all over the floor. Ava shook off the puddle of water and plucked off a rose from her arm.

"I fell into the vase." Ava giggled.

"Are you alright?"

"Just wet." Ava swiped at tears on her cheeks.

"Thank you," Simone said to the two staff members who came running at the commotion to clean up the mess.

"Here, let me." Quinn reached down, extending a hand to Ava.

Ava put her hands all over Quinn's biceps. "You're strong," she said.

Simone shook her head, wishing she had the confidence of her friend.

"Strong as I need to be. Ouch, that's some ring you have."

"It's the only ring I have." Ava giggled again and held out her hand, twisting the thick silver band, with the huge prongs, set around a red stone.

"Let me take you up to your room, Ava," Simone said, wanting Ava out of Quinn's arms.

Ava waved her off. "No, I'm good. Mielle's staying over. You go now."

"Ava, what a mess you made!" Mielle came over, grinning at them.

"Are you sure?" Simone asked as the other bridesmaid slung her arm over Ava.

"Oh, I have to support this double-dare," Mielle whispered as she passed Simone.

She and Ava giggled, and Simone's face grew hot.

"Looks like you're being pushed into my arms," he whispered into her ear.

She wasn't sure if she wanted to high-five her friends or hide in their hotel room.

"Bye, Simone! Have fun," Ava and Mielle called as the doors closed to their laughter.

"So, do you want to come to my place?" Quinn asked. Reaching out with his index finger, he slowly traced her jawline. Her hand came round his wrist, and she leaned into his touch.

She couldn't pass up a double-dare, could she? Or this gorgeous opportunity standing in front of her.

"I need to get a couple of things from my room," Simone said, turning out of Quinn's touch.

"Not so fast." His voice sent a shiver through her.

With a tug on her arm, Quinn embraced her hard, holding her against his solid chest, his hand on her neck. Simone's heart became a staccato as his lips met hers. He kissed like he danced in control. His tongue teased hers, and she followed his demand, her mouth opening to him.

"I've been waiting to do that since the moment I saw you."

Quinn traced her lips with his finger, and Simone quivered under his touch. "That was—"

"That's a taste of what's coming."

Heat raced through her and left her wanting more.

Simone flustered, backing away from him. "Meet you downstairs in the lobby?"

"I'll be waiting." Quinn's eyes bore into her. A tight knot of desire formed in Simone's body. She couldn't wait for Quinn to touch her again.

5

CHAPTER FIVE

When Quinn's eyes fell on Simone, and he took in how small and innocent she looked, he knew he wouldn't tell her about the threat, and a different plan took shape.

Watching her from across the room, seeing her laugh with her friends, taking in how that gown hugged her body just so and how composed she looked in the middle of the crowded ballroom, stirred something in him. A desire to have her under him. If he could seduce her and gain her trust, he could keep her safe while figuring out who'd hired him.

Maybe he was using Simone as a way of getting back on the horse. He snorted. The reasons didn't matter, someone had to keep her safe, and he was that someone.

He scanned the crowded lobby as he waited for Simone to come down, looking for anyone who stood out. If he could find out Simone's whereabouts from her social media posts, so could the people who wanted her harmed.

Then again, they had paid a fair sum to see him do it.

His eyes roamed over a man in a charcoal grey suit, who leaned against a chair. The man's eyes frantically darted back and forth until a tall woman with tears streaking down her face came from the hallway that led from the bathrooms. The man took a step forward, embraced the woman, and Quinn relaxed. Whatever that story was, he discarded it as a threat to Simone. The other groups of guests in the hotel came from the reception. As the elevator doors opened, Quinn strode towards Simone. That bridesmaid gown showed off the curve of her hips and breasts and emphasized her graceful neck.

"You brought your bag?" Quinn asked.

When she'd said she needed to go to her room to get a few things, he had thought of a purse, not a rolling suitcase.

Faint traces of pink bloomed across her cheeks.

Man, she looked so sweet when she blushed. He put his hand on her back and led her to a space near the reception desk.

"I planned to stay overnight, but it's late. I thought I would check out and go to my place from yours." With an effort, Quinn kept the frown off his face. If his sister went home with a strange man, he would want her to let a friend know. He hunched his shoulders. Simone's lack of attention to her personal safety annoyed him.

She gave him a small, tentative smile, her big brown eyes rising from the floor to meet his. "I told you, I've never gone home with a stranger before. I thought I might need stuff from my bag. Like clothes." He caressed her arms slowly, a smile spreading on his face. Her innocence and bravery in trusting him stirred his protective nature, and he wanted to shield her from the creep who was out to kill her more than anything.

"If you let me have my way with you, you won't need clothes," Quinn said in her ear and pulled her close. "Let your friends know where I'm taking you. If you give me your phone, I'll punch in the address and my cell number."

Simone dug through her purse and put a turquoise encased phone in his hand. "Thank you."

He punched in his details. "Here, send that to the other bridesmaid. Your friend Ava's too drunk to know what's going on. Tell her to check in with you in the morning," Quinn said.

Her eyes grew wide at his instructions, but she sent the text.

"Good girl. Ready for that drink?"

He caught how she smiled before ducking her head down to the floor. Quinn thought she might change her mind for a moment, but she squared her shoulders and took his hand.

When they stepped outside, Simone rubbed her arm. "Brrr!"

The pavement was slick from a soft rain, and Quinn held on to her as she stepped over the pebbled surface in her heels. As the sharp breeze hit them, another shiver rippled through her.

"Here." Quinn stopped and took off his suit jacket then settled it over her shoulders. He took the handle of her suitcase and stowed her luggage in the trunk. A jolt of electricity raced through him. This woman had caused his forgotten sex drive to stir to life. He couldn't wait to get her naked.

"We'll be there in a few minutes," Quinn opened the truck's door for her.

"Okay," Simone smiled, and his pulse raced.

He drove through the downtown streets passing the darkened shop windows. Simone's peach and vanilla scent teased his nostrils. Her phone buzzed. She frowned as she read it.

"Your friends checking in with you?" He asked.

"No. This is from an unknown number. I'm getting a lot of weird texts lately," Simone said. Her brow furrowed as she read the message.

His hands clutched the steering wheel.

"Weird how?" Quinn strived to keep his voice neutral. He didn't want to scare her.

"It's nothing, really." Simone put the phone back in her bag.

Quinn gritted his teeth. He needed to get his hands on her phone and see what those text messages were about.

The streetlights cast an orange glow off the glass of the shiny new building.

"That new Axis Management building definitely catches your eye." Simone leaned against the window, a look of concentration on her face.

"A stunning architectural achievement, according to the news." Quinn brushed his hand against her neck.

Done in contemporary metal, steel, and glass in varying shades of black, its bold design stood out.

"From the headlines about the actor's daughter who went missing, I know they're bodyguards to celebrities, but do they need an entire building for that?"

Quinn smiled. She wasn't the first to ask that question. The new building, formerly a depilated apartment complex, was how Xander showed his dick was the biggest in the private security game. Quinn drove around the corner and took the ramp into the underground parking.

"They do more than body guarding. Would you like to see inside?" Quinn asked.

"You work here?" asked Simone, her face blanched.

"Not at the moment. I'm staying in one of their guest suites," Quinn said.

Quinn placed a hand on her leg as she swallowed. Her bright gaze flashed to him, and Quinn braced himself for the question written on her face. "Did you work on the kidnapping of Grace Stevens' daughter?"

Quinn closed his eyes, pushing down the icy shivers Simone's question caused.

"If that's too personal, you don't have to talk about it," Simone said.

"No, it's fine." Quinn stared straight ahead, out the windshield.

Except he didn't talk about it. He hadn't in the last four months. It was why he'd quit working for Axis Management as leader of their Team Stealth. He tried to quit altogether. His bosses didn't accept his resignation. They were convinced he was taking a break. He needed Simone to trust him, not find out how he got his best friend killed.

"Yes. I worked on Mulberry Stevens' case." His chest felt as tight as his voice.

She reached up, softly brushing his hair out of his eyes with her fingertips. Quinn startled.

"That must have been horrible," Simone said.

The compassionate gaze in her eyes, her soothing touch, made him want to bolt. Using all his strength to focus, he grabbed her hand, dropping light feathering kisses on it. Simone giggled.

"Yeah, it wasn't fun."

Axis Management kept their cases out of the press, but somehow the disappearance of renowned actor Grace Stevens' daughter got into the media.

What the press didn't know was Jordan had lost his life on that job, all because of Quinn's fuck-up. He'd been the leader of the private operative team, and he took that responsibility seriously.

Quinn shifted in his seat, holding her hand.

"Want to see inside?"

"That has to be a million-dollar view for sure," Simone said.

Quinn held his breath as an expression of doubt flickered across her face. Her berry lips spread in a tentative smile.

Fuck, yeah. We're getting somewhere. He squeezed her hand.

"Yes, I want to see inside," she said.

With her fluttering movements and the small traces of confidence he gleamed, she reminded him of a little bird. A bird wanting to take the chance and fly.

Her small hand was warm as he took it in his and guided her through the personal door and up through the stairwell. Inside the black and steel building, black tiles gleamed in the low light. He paused, noticing a light on in the reception area.

"Come inside here. I want to check on a friend." Quinn opened the glass doors that led to the reception area and abruptly froze as he caught sight of a willowy brunette sitting behind a computer screen, blinking up at him in surprise.

"Harper, what are you doing here so late?" He glared at Xander's assistant as she flashed him a smile.

"All of you Club Bandit men are the same overprotective cavemen. A meeting went late, and the cleaners finished half an hour ago. Xander got called away and asked me to stay until they finished, and I got caught sending everyone the new layouts. I worked down here instead of opening the upstairs office again."

"He works you too hard," Quinn said, his glare easing into a smile.

"Tell *him* that." Harper rolled her eyes. "I love your show! I catch it whenever I can," she said to Simone.

"Thanks." Simone blushed.

"How are you getting home?" Quinn asked.

"Waiting for Logan to pick me up and take me to breakfast." A crimson flush stained Harper's cheeks. Quinn raised his eyebrows but refrained from commenting further and took Simone's arm. "Have fun," he called over his shoulder.

Harper smiled, gave them a wave, and returned to her computer screens.

Quinn took them down a hallway to an opened elevator.

As soon as the doors closed, he pulled Simone close to him, kissing her hard. He closed his eyes and breathed in her scent, her softness a balm to his grief-weary soul. He broke off the kiss before he ripped off her clothes right here.

The elevator doors opened. He took her hand in his and walked her down the plush carpeted hallway to the suite door.

"What's Club Bandit?"

"Club Bandit is a private BDSM Club. Bandit Brothers is how some of the founding members refer to themselves."

Stopping beside the door, he pinned her to the wall. The hitch in her breathing made him hard.

"Don't suppose you have ever been?"

Taking her fingers in his, he kissed the back of her hand.

"To a BDSM Club? No, I didn't know one existed in this city. I like dance clubs, and once I went to a—a burlesque show," Simone stammered, her eyes looking everywhere except his face.

Gently, he slid his hand down her cheek. How she looked away then looked right at him made him want to push her a little more.

"But you've been curious?"

"About a club I didn't know existed?" She smiled shyly.

Quinn swiped the keycard, laughing. "Not what I meant, pretty girl. Come on in." He held the door open and let her go ahead of him.

The large space with its deep green walls and the oversized black leather sectional that hugged the far wall, with the giant TV screen opposite the sectional, screamed masculinity. Simone circled the room, her gaze taking in all of it.

"Two bedrooms down the hall." Quinn gestured. He took off his suit jacket and hung it in the front closet.

"You weren't kidding about the view." Simone gestured towards the window.

"I'm just borrowing the digs," Quinn said.

"This is stunning." Simone's eyes went big, taking in the place.

"I would rather look at you," Quinn said. He took a step towards her, put his hands on her shoulders, massaging them gently. As the tension left her body and Simone relaxed against him, he pressed his lips to the back of her neck, breathing in her peach and vanilla scent.

With his hands on her hips, he moved her towards the plane of glass.

"I want you naked against this glass, watching as your body climaxes." He nibbled at her ear.

"I—I have never..." Simone stuttered, looking away from him.

"Feel how hard the sight of you makes me." He brought her hand to the front of his tented slacks. Simone bit her lip. Her hand trembled, her brown eyes darted left and right.

Damn, he'd pushed too far; she was looking for an escape. Time to reel it in. He took her hand in his, kissing her lips softly.

"We'll take it slow," he said and led her over to the sectional.

"I'm nervous," Simone said.

Her apprehensive expression tugged at his heart. Quinn brushed a hand over her honey locks.

"We won't do anything you don't want to. Sit, I'll get refreshments."

He opened the fridge and took out a bowl of grapes and a prepared cheese board then set both down on the coffee table. After that, he brought over two glasses of sparkling water.

"Thank you." Simone's hand shook as she accepted the glass he offered.

"So, how did you come to have fantasies about being tied up?" He sat right beside her, putting an arm around her shoulders.

Yeah, the question shocked her, and Quinn couldn't keep the smile off his face. Never had he been with a woman inexperienced in kink, and the thought of having a novice sent the blood to his cock. A tingle of desire hummed at the base of his spine. She put the water glass down, her fingers trembling slightly.

"In college, I went to a girl's night out with Ava and Meredith, where someone was selling sex toys. That was the first time I saw a vibrator, and I got curious."

That blush of hers, so sweet and innocent as it surged across her cheeks. Quinn shifted on the cushion, nudging her legs open with his foot.

"How did you know you wanted to be the one tied-up, not the one who ties?"

Under his arm, Simone squirmed and covered her face with her hands.

Quinn laughed softly, his hand gently lifting her fingers off her face. "No hiding. You can tell me. You've come this far," he said. He took her hand in his and stroked the spot between her index finger and thumb.

Simone shifted away from him, her gaze locked on the floor. He applied just a little more pressure on her hand, and she shifted back towards him.

"I couldn't stop thinking about it, and it led me to some books on BDSM and D/s," she murmured.

"But you've never tried it?"

"No. My ex-husband thought anything kinky was perverted," Simone said. The sadness in her eyes gnawed at him.

Her ex sounded like a douche bag. He needed to check him out, pronto. What kind of man would refuse to explore when his wife brought up being kinky?

"He's wrong." He hooked his foot around her leg, bringing her closer. "Kinky can be sexy as hell."

He tightened his arm around her as a shudder racked through her body.

"How did you know you wanted to be the one to tie up women?"

Quinn shrugged. "For me, when I discovered kink, it was obvious which side I wanted to be on. Anyone can pick up a flogger, Simone. It's the power exchange that has always interested me."

Back when he'd found life interesting.

"You like telling people what to do?"

Yeah, he couldn't help it.

"I think I'm good at telling people what to do. When it comes to D/s, it's the thought of a woman giving up her power and letting me take charge that I'm interested in. To cause a woman to crave my touch, to wring every ounce of pleasure out of her, that's why this interests me."

Slowly, he wrapped his hand through her honey strands, tugging on them just a bit.

"So more than floggers and ordering someone around." She squirmed on the cushion.

"Much more." Quinn traced a finger along her lower lip. "Why did you go solo at the wedding?"

The change of conversation caught her off guard, as he intended, causing her to stop shifting. She looked at him and he smiled.

"I haven't dated since the break-up of my marriage." A forlorn expression crossed her face, and Quinn shifted even closer to her.

"How long were you married?"

"Three years. Six months since it ended." The pain in her voice made him want to stab something on her behalf.

"What about you? Why did you come solo?" she asked.

"With my work, I don't stay in one place long enough, so relationships aren't my thing."

Best to say that right away. He didn't want Simone to think a long-term relationship was possible.

He smiled as she leaned into his touch, letting the soft strands fall from his fingertips.

"What about your work? What do you enjoy about it?"

"I enjoy showing people how to make their spaces better. It makes me happy."

"But you're shy about it."

Simone squirmed, moving forward on the cushion. "Honestly, I'm not comfortable telling people."

The woman appeared on television every morning and had for the last year, but she was uncomfortable with it?

"I bet that makes you very popular for suitors," Quinn said.

"I don't think I'm ready to date again." Simone put a hand on his leg.

"What about some play?" Quinn said. He brought her onto his lap, laughing at her wide-eyed expression. "But, Simone, for play to work between us, you have to be honest."

Quinn rubbed her neck with the flat of his hand and circled her breasts through the rich material of her gold dress.

A giggle slipped out, and she touched her fingertips to her lips. "Yes, I would like to try some play." He cupped a hand to the back of her neck, sucking at her bottom lip. Damn, the sweet taste of her sent a wave of electric heat through him. He wanted more.

Simone jerked back, and Quinn tightened his hold on her.

"How long has it been for you since you had sex?"

She twisted away from him. He tightened his hold on the back of her neck slightly, wanting to push her more.

"That's personal," her hands pressed down on his legs

"Simone, tell me," he added a touch of dominance to his tone.

"We didn't have much of a sex life."

"Why?" Her ex had to be half dead.

Simone shrugged. "Doesn't matter."

"I want to take you to bed, fuck you, and make you scream, but I don't want to hurt you. When's the last time you've had sex? This is part of being honest and open."

She met his eyes, and his cock stirred. He knew he had her.

"A year and six months."

He wanted to take her back to the bedroom and show her how good kink could be. His balls tightened at the thought.

"What do you say to a bit of play right now?" he asked, his voice thick.

He stroked her hair, looked into those big brown eyes, cupped her face with his hands, and kissed those berry pink lips. The taste of her, fresh and sweet, eased his tension. He couldn't wait to have more.

6

—•—

CHAPTER SIX

Simone slowly eased herself off Quinn's lap, her stomach in a tangled knot as she stood in front of him.

"Simone, what is it?" he asked his gentle tone at odds with his muscular build. He took her hand in his.

If she told him, he would think her a tease. But if this was as far as they went, she owed him an explanation. Quinn took both her hands in his strong ones and raised an eyebrow. He didn't look as if he scared easily.

"You know, good girls don't go home with strange men." She focused on a point on the wall, so she didn't have to see his expression. He would probably laugh at her.

"We won't do anything you don't want to do. Have you heard of SSC?" Quinn said.

After puzzling over the acronym for a moment, she took her head and leaned back against his chest, liking the comfort of his solid body.

"As a Dom, it's my responsibility to make sure you are safe. I adhere to SSC, which stands for Safe, Sane, and Consensual. Is there something I can do to make you feel safe?" Quinn stood, still holding her hands in his. He wrapped his arms around her, bringing her to his hard chest. God, it felt so good to be in his arms.

Shaking her head, Simone leaned against him. Her pulse raced, but she wasn't afraid. Nervous, yes. But not afraid. Realizing that, the knot in her stomach untangled. Safety obviously meant something to him. She hadn't even thought of letting her friends know she had left with Quinn, a strange man—a total modern woman failure. But he'd thought of it.

"Can I ask you another question?" Simone asked.

"You can ask twenty." So sexy how his lips did that turning-up-at-the-corners thing.

"What's your last name?"

"Walsh."

"How old are you, Quinn Walsh?"

"Twenty-six," he said. His hands massaged her shoulders.

"You're easing away my worries." How would his hands feel on her naked skin? She needed to find out.

"Let's play," Quinn said. "Ready?"

"Yes," Simone said.

His smile lit his blue eyes like a summer's day clearing after a storm. He held out his hand. She took it and ambled with him down the carpeted hallway to a closed door.

"Anything else you want to know?" His hand rested on the knob.

"No," Simone said, her mind made up.

This wasn't just about sex. She wanted to experience what she had spent countless lonely nights fantasizing about.

"After you." He opened the door, motioned her to step in before him.

Unlike the rest of the suite, this bedroom screamed afterthought. She smoothed her hand over the soft sheets, contemplated what colour she would paint those white plaster walls. Maybe a rosy beige or sage green.

"This could use some work." She turned on her designer brain to tamp down her nerves, ignoring the four-poster king bed.

"It's a crash pad. Those of us who use it sleep very little." He leaned on the door; the heat of this scrutiny raised goosebumps along her flesh, uncomfortable but powerful.

"I don't know what to do." She fidgeted with her gown. A man like him had to be used to experienced women. Not a divorcee who'd hardly had sex during the entirety of her marriage. But her ex-husband had never watched her the way Quinn tracked every inch of her body with his eyes.

"Simone." His voice, calm but steely. "Put yourself in my hands. For one night, can you trust me?"

He wasn't asking for her undying trust—just one night.

"Yes, Quinn." She meant it, wanting what he offered. Her heart fluttered as he swallowed up her personal space.

"Should we find out what's going to turn you on, Simone?" His sultry tone made her pussy twitch.

No one had ever tried to discover what made her orgasm before. Liam viewed sex as a legal requirement to seal their marriage.

"I don't know," she admitted shyly.

"By your dilated eyes and your shallow breath, I can see how much you want this." Quinn leaned down, captured her lips with his, and Simone's pulsed raced. He let go abruptly, then traced a finger along the column on her neck, sliding down around her breast over her silky gown. Her throat went dry as his touch seared her. Simone bit her lip to keep in the moan. He palmed her breasts. His hands, rough against the fabric, sent her nerves firing with heated anticipation. Over her gown, his touch felt so good. She leaned into it, anticipating what it would feel like on her bare skin.

"We'll take it slow," he murmured. "If I ask you to do something that makes you uncomfortable, say, 'yellow,' and I'll check in with you. If I'm doing something you don't like, say, 'red,' and I'll stop immediately. We'll talk about why you said 'red' and go from there. I'm in control as long as you surrender to me. The power of refusal lies with you," Quinn said.

Simone nodded. From her reading about BDSM, she had come across safe words, which reassured her that they were real safety measures.

"What happens if I say 'green'?"

"We keep going." Quinn grinned.

It sounded terrifying and thrilling and exactly what she wanted but hadn't known she could get. Until now.

Simone mewled as his lips grazed her collarbone, glided down the hollow of her throat

"Do you know what I think a good girl is?"

"What?" Simone bit her lip.

"A girl who asks for what she craves. Tell me the fantasy you want fulfilled, right here and now."

She couldn't meet his eyes. Quinn took her chin in his fingers.

"I told you what I wanted," Simone said. Saying it would expose her. The memory of being rejected for her desires was still a fresh wound.

"Consent is sexy. Tell me what you want tonight," Quinn said. He crushed her against him.

"Tie me to the bed." Saying the words, embarrassed her. Not quite embarrassed, saying them out loud, was a thrill that made her panties wet.

As he took a step towards her, a hot flush broke out across her skin.

"How many climaxes do you think I can make you have?"

Quinn closed the space between them, pressed his hands on either side of her face, and his tongue invaded her mouth, dominating hers. Reaching up, she cupped his face, feeling his rough whiskered skin. Simone shuddered, so completely intimate, touching this stranger.

She swallowed. Her face was on fire. She had a vibe in the sock drawer, and she used it, but being with a man, this sexy, confident man, who wanted to give her pleasure, thrilled her.

Quinn's icy blues blazed into her, searing her flesh. "I can't wait to fix that. By the time I'm done with you, you're going to have so many you'll wonder how you lived without them." He took a step back. "Strip."

She trembled slightly, but her pussy surged at the command. She wanted this so much, it surprised and shocked her. Yet she couldn't help but give in to the intensity in his eyes, the sure command of his tone.

Simone reached behind her neck, undoing the clasp. Slowly, she stepped out of the gold bridesmaid gown. Her fingers trembling, she pulled down the nylons. She bit her lip. Her fingertips paused at the hem of her lacy panties.

"Those too." Quinn nodded.

Simone stepped out of the panties and tossed them towards her other clothes. She unclasped the front closure of her bra, letting it fall. She stood naked with a man she just met. Her pulse raced. No going back now.

"Nice." Quinn trailed his index finger over her collarbone, tracing a lazy circle around each breast. As he stared at her, her nipples became points of heated need she wanted him to touch. Her pulse sped up, her breath came out in quick gasps as Quinn's hands held her breasts, his thumbs brushing over her nipples. He cradled them as if they were precious. The heat from his touch made her shiver.

"They're so small," Simone said.

"They're perfect," Quinn said. He squeezed them. The calluses on his hands felt abrasive against her delicate skin, Simone threw her head back and closed her eyes.

"You like the pressure?" Quinn asked, squeezing and twisting her nipples.

"Yes," Simone breathed out.

"Can't wait to have clamps on these pretty nipples," he said.

Quinn let go of her breasts and slid his hands along her ass; he moved his finger further down and idly tapped above her mound.

"Spread your legs. Let me feel your pussy."

She spread as wide as she could, her toes digging into the carpet.

"How do you feel?" Quinn asked, his voice deep and husky.

"Afraid of my...legs giving out." Talking was becoming an effort.

"Trust me. I got you." He placed a hand on the small of her back. "Now open more"

Simone leaned into his feverish hand and spread wider. She gasped as his fingers circled her swollen clit, and without warning, he plunged two fingers deep into her core. Rocking against him, her nerve endings fired, spilling wicked heat through her veins.

As quickly as he entered her, he pulled his fingers out. She bit back a moan as Quinn held his fingers in front of her face. She smelled the tangy aroma of her arousal.

"Open your mouth," he commanded.

The weight of his finger on her bottom lip caused her pulse to pound in her ears. She tasted the saltiness of her juices, as he rubbed his finger back and forth along her lip.

"That's a pretty submissive," Quinn said.

His finger moved in and out of her mouth, Simone's hands clasped around his arms.

"I need to taste you," he murmured.

Pulling his finger out of her mouth, he circled the tip of her nipple, then the other one.

"Taste?"

He kneeled in front of her and bringing her close to him, so his whiskered face felt gritty against her skin. He slowly licked her nipple, lapping it as if it was a tasty dessert. She arched towards him, moaning. Somehow, he looked even more powerful being on his knees in front of her.

"That's it. Make those sounds," Quinn instructed. He licked and lapped, and wetness pooled between her legs all over again. His teeth grazed the tip of her nipple. The jolt of pain sent shock waves down her legs. Her hands went to his soft dark hair.

"God, Quinn." Simone arched back, his hand firmly on her back, kept her there. "Too much!" Simone cried.

His fingers circled her clit, slowly. Then he sank one finger in her centre, and she gasped as he thrust another digit deep inside her. As he increased his speed, pleasure built in her core, turning her face against his wall of muscles, his shirt soft on her cheek, her hands fisted.

"I don't think I can keep standing," Simone said.

"Yes, you can." His tone said not only could she, but she would.

His finger curled deeply inside, hitting her G-spot. Her muscles contracted, and her legs shook. A scream tore from her throat as the orgasm rolled through her and she collapsed against his strong forearm.

"Look how you came for me, how your body responded to each of my commands. Stunning." He stroked her hair.

Her thoughts floated in her mind, her body boneless.

"Come here." His powerful arms held her.

She breathed in his woodsy, clean scent until it filled her. "I didn't expect that," she said, her voice shaky.

"We're just getting started." Quinn's eyes bore into hers, and he kissed her as if he never wanted to stop. He stood up, raised an eyebrow at her. "I believe someone asked to be tied to the bed?"

"Yes," Simone said. Her heart galloped, sweat gathered on her hands.

"Get on the bed, Simone," Quinn said.

Simone bit her lip. *I'm already naked. I can do this.* Exhaling the pent up breath she was holding, she laid down.

"Now should we go the classic spread eagle? Or hands and feet?" Quinn trailed his fingers along her calf to her hip, sparking sensations all along her.

"Whatever you want," Simone said.

God, where did those words come from?

For a moment, Quinn stilled.

"Bring her your together for me."

Simone did, feeling silly. Quinn reached over, kissed her ear. "Stay exactly like that."

"Yes, Quinn," she said. As she concentrated on doing what he asked, a thrill of anticipation raced through her.

Her breath caught in her throat as he rummaged in a large leather bag. Simone's throat grew dry as she saw the end of a flogger. Quinn pulled out a bundle of black rope. Slowly, he wrapped the soft black rope around her wrists.

"There's more to this than I thought," Simone said.

"Think of this as an intro," he said. The rope ended up being between her wrists. Quinn pulled her wrists so her arms were above her head. A moment later, she felt the rope tighten, but not comfortably so, as he tied it off to the bedpost.

"How do you feel?"

Simone licked her lips. "Bare." *Exposed. Vulnerable.*

He held all the power, leaving her completely at his mercy, and she liked it.

His gigantic hands caressed her calves, slowly tying the rope above her ankle. With every pass of rope, it felt tighter but in a good way.

"Going to leave your legs free, because I want them around me," he said.

He leaned down, his lips tickling the backs of her calves, trailing soft whiskery kisses from her thigh to her ankle.

"If it feels too tight, tell me," Quinn said, pulling on the rope above her head.

"Okay," Simone said.

Her thoughts halted as his hands cupped her breasts. She yelped as he pinched a nipple between his thumb and index finger. A moan escaped from low in the back of her throat. As he pinched the other nipple, her hips arched. Simone bit the inside of her cheek as the coil of pressure mounted. The heat in his eyes scorched her.

"Good girls make noise. I want to hear all your sounds." From her throat to her breasts, he kissed her. Each pass of his lips made the ache in her core hungry for attention.

He moved from the bed, taking the heat and comfort with him.

"I'm right here." He grinned at her from beside the bed.

He ripped his shirt off, revealing the V-tapered muscles she remembered being under earlier in the night. "Are you impatient?"

"No. Maybe?"

Quinn laughed, his hands unzipping the fly on his dress pants, slowly freeing his well-toned legs. She couldn't move her eyes from his erect, thick cock. Butterflies tightened in her tummy as she wondered how he was going to fit in her. From the nightstand, he grabbed a condom and rolled it on.

"Damn, you're a very pretty submissive."

She blushed; the praise formed a knot of desire in her belly. His dusting of chest hair tickled her nipples as he braced over her on his forearms. He kissed her lips until they felt swollen. Deep in her core, desire blazed, her mind emptied of all her insecurities as he worked his way down her body, nipping, leaving a trail of kisses down her ribcage. She gasped as his teeth scraped across her inner thigh. Her fingertips stretched in the ropes, digging in her palm, desperately reaching for a contrast against the overwhelming pleasure. His wet tongue flicked once, twice, against her clit.

"Stunning." Quinn stared at her body with admiration, and she liked the attention.

She moaned as he blew hot air over her clit. He gripped each thigh, and her body trembled as he slowly licked the length of her.

"Yes!" The low moan vibrated from somewhere far away. Heat engulfed her as his tongue pressed against her clit.

"God, Quinn!" The fire in her body grew hotter, the coil wound tighter. Her eyes opened as he stopped.

"Keep your eyes on me. Watch as I make you come." His voice banked that heat in her and her hips arched as much as the rope would allow.

She didn't know if she could. The heated pleasure made her eyelids heavy. In a far corner of her mind, she doubted her body could have another orgasm, but her clit ached with emptiness. She wanted his tongue back there.

"That's a good submissive." He bent down, his dark hair back in between her legs, and Simone felt the tension uncoil as his hot mouth covered her clit, his tongue back on her clit. She kept her eyes open. Simone screamed as his teeth graze her clit, his tongue pressing on her bud, giving even pressure. His hands squeezed her thighs. "God, Quinn!" The orgasm towed her under; her vision blurred.

Her head went dizzy as the flame consumed her body.

"You look so perfect. That's two," Quinn smiled.

Goosebumps rose on her arms, and heat swelled from her centre. His face, a breath from hers, his piercing blue eyes imprisoned her. He smiled slowly before his lips crashed into hers. She tasted herself on his tongue and mewled. His powerful rough hands slid down the curve of her ribcage to her hips until his fingers grabbed her thighs.

"Ask me to fuck you."

She couldn't form the words. The fear of rejection rearing its ugly head.

"Simone."

Overriding the insecurity was the knowledge she knew this man would never reject her.

He had just given her everything she had hoped for.

"Please, fuck me, Quinn."

God, there was so much heat in her body as his lips crashed against hers. His hand grabbed her ass, grabbing and pinching.

"I want your legs over my shoulders," Quinn directed.

He helped her get settled, and the position made her arms feel more stretched, but it wasn't uncomfortable.

The way he looked at her sent fiery sparks through her. She ached to clutch the bedsheets; her bound hands preventing her.

With his cock in hand, he entered her inch by inch. God, she never thought sex could be like this, a treasure trove of sensations. Another inch and her walls gripped him. Slowly, he slid out again.

"Quinn!" God, the neediness overwhelmed her.

"Making sure you're ready." He flashed that wicked smile at her, and her insides melted.

"You warmed me up just right," Simone said.

"That was the plan." He slid into her again, kissing her mouth, swallowing her cries as he started to thrust, long and slow.

She cried out nonsensical words as he thrust, long and slow. He sank in deeper, stroking her.

It felt so good. Lost in the rhythm of his thrusts, his face contorted, his body tensed. He was the sexiest thing she had ever seen, with taut abs, the wall of muscle and yet, he tenderly held her legs, lifting her hips.

"Simone," he called out.

One longer thrust, and he let go, his face relaxing as his orgasm rolled through him.

He called my name. A live current of thrill shot through her body. She was bound, but something about his release made her feel powerful. Not like she had the power over him. Very clearly, he was the Dom. As the heat in his eyes roamed over her, Simone shuddered. Wanted. Feeling wanted, she realized, was powerful.

"Quinn." God, he looked so incredibly hot and masculine.

"Absolutely beautiful. You did so well." He kissed her softly.

"That was nice," Simone said and cringed.

Nice? That's the best I can do after he gave me the best orgasms of my life?

"Let's get you out of these ropes," he said.

Mesmerized, she watched as he deftly untied her wrists, taking her arm in his hands and rubbing small circles.

"Thank you."

"My pleasure." Quinn kissed her softly. "I'll be right back."

She turned on her side, watched him move across the floor to the bathroom, the tight muscles of his ass rippling with each step.

She smiled as he removed the condom, washed his hands, and came back with a washcloth.

"What's that for?"

"For you. Spread."

A flush of embarrassment rolled through her as he gently wiped her pussy.

"I want to do that again."

Laughter lit his face, making him look younger.

"Come back tonight. I can show you more. Now, rest."

"Okay."

His arms came around her and held her tight. "I've got you."

As she snuggled against him in a strange bed after having her first-ever one-night stand, her body hummed in satisfaction.

7

CHAPTER SEVEN

For the first time in months, Quinn slept over four hours straight. At eight am as he chopped up vegetables and grated cheese, he even caught himself smiling. Widely.

Maybe it wasn't just the continuous sleep. The openness and trust Simone gave soothed his knotted grief. Her expression locked in pleasure came front and centre in his mind, how her eyes glowed, how the smile spread slowly on her face as her fingers ran through his hair, down the side of his face. Quinn's mouth ached from smiling. She gave him submission. He could give her breakfast.

His smile faded as he thought of Rachel.

Quinn knew he should have ended it sooner, and he regretted how he'd treated her.

Rachel needed a firm hand with parameters that he wasn't interested in giving. He hadn't realized she was a masochist. He'd thought her just a brat. Maybe she was both. Years of looking after other people took the appeal out of beating a sub into submission. He hadn't fully realized that until last night when Simone willingly took all that he gave her.

He pressed start on the coffeemaker, and the sound of the bedroom door closing took him down the hall.

And he hadn't realized he wanted a sub who could do the laundry while wearing his shirt until now.

He let out a low whistle. Simone smiled at him, loading the washing machine, wearing nothing but his dress shirt from the night before. The sight sent all the blood racing to his cock.

"Good morning."

"What a sexy sight you are." He put his hands on her waist, kissing the back of her neck. He smiled as her cheeks reddened.

"It seemed the least I could do."

"You don't owe me anything."

"No, it's not... the sheets needed a wash, and then I saw there was a pile of laundry in the hamper. It's not a big deal."

"Thanks."

As her hand hit the start button, he lifted it and kissed her fingers.

"You are too tempting." He wondered if he could get her ass red to match her face. "I want to spank you."

Nuzzling her neck, dropping a line of kisses around the hollow of her throat, he felt her quiver under his touch.

"Because I did your laundry?"

"Exactly."

His hand slid and cupped her ass. He kneaded the round globe with one hand, pinching it. "Because you doing laundry for me while wearing nothing but my shirt is the hottest thing I have ever seen. My cock is hard for you. Put your hands on the back of the washing machine and lean forward."

She bit her lip. Then her big brown eyes met his, silently asking him for reassurance.

"You told me last night you fantasized about being flogged. Did you ever wonder about a spanking?"

"Yes."

"Turn around, lean forward, and put your hands on the back of the washer."

She did, without complaint.

Damn it. This woman did things to him, and he loved it, but he was in trouble.

"Beautiful."

As his hands ran down her back, under his shirt, over the smooth skin of her bottom, his balls drew tight.

He landed one solid smack on her right cheek, admiring the spot of pink it left, swiftly landed another.

Simone yelped.

"How was that?"

"That was fine."

Quinn grabbed the flesh of her ass. "Fine is not acceptable. I want to know how you feel when I ask you."

"It hurt."

He danced his fingers along her tailbone.

"The correct response is 'May I have another, Quinn?'"

With a sly smile, she wiggled her behind.

"May I have another, Quinn?"

"My pleasure."

His hand vibrated with the warmth of her ass as he alternated his swats left and right. She writhed and cried out but kept her hands on the washer. His palm connected with her flesh for one more swat, and Simone yelped.

He had missed the sound of his hand on a woman's bare flesh. "Good girl."

Slowly, he rubbed each ass cheek, admiring how her body arched toward his. He gathered her hair in his hands, and he kissed her neck.

She whimpered, and he slid his shirt off her shoulders.

"How do you feel?"

"Good."

"Wet?"

At her nod, Quinn slid a finger in her folds.

"I enjoy making you wet."

From over her shoulder, her thick eyelashes lifted, her smile fuelled him.

His hand pressed to the base of her spine, circled her puckered hole.

"Are you an anal virgin?"

As she leaned back against him, Quinn put a hand under her chin, titling her face until her eyes grew wide. He knew he could lose himself in those depths.

"Yes, Quinn."

"Have you been curious about what it would feel like to have a cock buried deep there?" Nope, the blush on her cheeks is redder than the colour on her ass.

"Maybe."

"Another time." Quinn kissed her pillowy lips, skimmed his hands under her breasts, and grabbed them, pressing his thumbs over her nipples.

He guided her arms so they were out in front of her, her fingertips on the back of the washing machine.

"Don't move, or I'll spank you so hard you won't be able to sit. Clear?"

"Clear," Simone said.

Damn this woman. He couldn't help but push her a bit more to see what her reaction would be. In the bathroom, he grabbed a condom from the box in the cabinet and came back to her, taking a moment to admire the picture she made, perfectly arched over the washing machine, exactly as he'd left her.

"Good girl."

Quinn caught the scent of her arousal and knew he would not last long. He rolled on the condom and slowly rubbed his cock along her entrance.

Simone let out the softest little whimper.

From behind her, he stretched his fingers and played with both of her nipples while circling her clit with his other hand.

"Tell me you want this."

"Please fuck me, Quinn."

Her voice was almost guttural. He nipped her earlobe and thumbed her clit hard.

"Give me your noises, baby."

With one thrust, his cock seated deep in her fiery core and desire tightened his balls.

Crying out, Simone arched towards him, and he gritted his teeth. Sweat broke on his back, and her juices soaked his fingers.

She bucked against him, and he laughed. "Keep that up."

Increasing his rhythm, he pinched her clit.

He groaned as her pussy clenched around him, and with one deep long stroke, he dove into her warm core as her pussy walls gripped him. He brought a forearm across her chest for support as he rocked in her, balls deep. Damn, her liquid heat enveloped him, and he groaned.

"You are so damn tight, Simone."

"Quinn!"

His name from her lips urged him on; his own orgasm claimed him.

As Simone panted under him, with her hands stretched out on the washing machine, Quinn wanted to stay buried in her forever. "That was delicious."

Simone giggled.

He grabbed her hair and kissed the back of her neck before dislodging from her heat and discarding the condom. "Think I'll have you do my laundry naked forever now."

"I might be up for it once in a while."

Her forest floor eyes seared him, and his heart beat wildly, his hands unsteady. This woman threw him out of his carefully constructed box. He took a few steps back, putting physical distance between them.

"I'm going to have a shower. Someone has done naughty things to me."

He swatted her ass. "Clean towels and everything you need is on the shelves. I have more naughty things to show you."

"Can't wait."

She kissed him, her lips feathery soft on his.

"Go now or you might not make it to that shower."

Simone closed the door, and Quinn momentarily regretted not starting in there. Then, with one look at the washing machine, he grinned.

****

"Coffee?"

Simone stood in front of Quinn in kitten heels, a linen skirt, and a red tunic. *Damn, she's too classy for my worn-out self.*

"Yes. Oh wow. You cook?"

"Yeah," Quinn shrugged. He had been cooking since he could reach the stove.

"I am the worst cook. I can barely make things from a box. I'm lucky I don't have to cook for the show. I just show people where things go in their kitchen," Simone said.

"Do you like your job? You seem uncomfortable with your fame." His fingers brushed hers as he passed her the coffee mug.

"I kind of fell into it. The show just happened to me but it's not a big deal."

Quinn's chest tightened. Someone planned to kill her, and the most likely motivation behind that was tied to her show.

"You probably don't watch it," Simone said, sliding the coffee mug between her hands.

"Don't make assumptions," Quinn grinned at her. "So, you didn't learn to cook growing up?"

"No, we had a cook."

Quinn couldn't imagine Simone in either of his childhood kitchens. The middle-class setting didn't suit her.

"What do your parents do?"

"My dad was a surgeon. He died a month after I married Liam. My mother was the CFO of a charity. She died when I was eight."

He passed her a plate and sat on the stool beside hers. He ran his knuckles over her cheek. "I'm sorry you lost them."

She took a sip of coffee, shrugged her shoulders. "Thanks. I was close to my dad, though he could be suffocating."

"Ah. Suffocating how?"

Simone twirled a golden piece of hair around her fingers, tucking it behind her ear. She shrugged, not meeting his eyes. "I was all he had, so most of my upbringing was sheltered. He had old-fashioned ideas."

"Like no sex before marriage?" Quinn asked. Damn, the way her cheeks instantly flushed when she was uncomfortable was so adorable.

"Like that. What about your parents?"

Not his favourite subject. He shifted on the stool. But sharing was part of the deal for building trust. "My dad is a carpenter." *And a decent one when John wasn't hitting the bottle.*

"And your mom?"

"She paints." It was like saying Usain Bolt jogged, but he didn't like to talk about Deirdre.

"Are you close to them?"

"Not really. Did your ex cook?"

"A little." Simone moved food around her plate.

"Why did it end between you two?"

Her shoulders hunched forward, and he took her hand and rubbed his thumb over her slender fingers.

"When we first met, Liam had a passion for his work. He's a mineralogist, and he would talk about all the cool trips we would go on and research papers he was writing. Almost overnight, he lost interest and became detached. From me and also from the business he had with a friend. He withdrew."

"He sounds like an asshole."

She smiled.

"Now he builds houses in Peru or something. He up and left one day. His business partner wasn't happy about it either."

Her phone buzzed. Simone looked at it, frowned, and put it down again.

"Why did you marry him?"

"My dad wanted to see me married before he died. Liam seemed interesting and kind, so when he asked me to marry him, I said yes and stuck it out for three unhappy years."

"That sounds awful."

"There are worse things."

Yeah, but his heart rate increased at the thought of her spending three years being unhappy. The first chance he got, he would check out her ex. Maybe he wasn't as detached as he seemed.

Her phone buzzed again.

"Is that work? Do you have to leave?"

"No, it's nothing."

His instincts told him otherwise. She'd received texts last night, on their way home from the reception. With Rachel, she would have hidden the phone from him, called him names, and stomped her foot.

Curious to see how Simone would react, Quinn put out his hand.

"Give me your phone."

Without hesitation, she put the phone in his hand.

"Good girl."

At his praise, her cheeks flushed, her pulse raced at the hollow of her throat. This woman did things to him. He growled and wondered again how she could be so careless with her safety.

"Have you reported these?"

"No. I didn't think they were a big deal."

"Die bitch," he read in as toneless a voice as he could. "Sweetheart, these are threats."

The colour drained from her face. He wished he could have softened the words, but he needed her to take her security seriously.

"They're just text messages."

"I'll be right back." He dropped a kiss on those berry lips.

In the spare room, he called Xander and filled in his former boss and friend. He ended the call and smiled, watching her wash the dishes, but he noticed the tension in her body his words had caused.

Quinn wished he could protect her from every threat against her. If mere text messages affected her like this, it was clear she couldn't handle knowing the real danger she was in. This wasn't her line of work. It was his, even though he wanted to escape it, he couldn't walk away and leave her.

"Have you got any fan mail like those text messages?" he handed her phone back. "Anyone upset with you at work?"

"Lots from people saying they like the show or companies asking me to use their products. And my circle is small. I can't think of anyone who is upset or angry."

"Anyone new hanging around your office?"

"No, we have security at the studio."

Quinn scoffed. Even the best security couldn't stop someone determined to stalk.

"I love the show, but the demographic is women in their late thirties to fifties. I honestly think these texts are a prank or spam or something."

"These texts aren't random."

Simone dried her hands on a kitchen towel.

"I show quick tips on how you can make a room comfortable, how you can spruce up your bathroom on a budget. I don't think anyone feels threatened by it."

"Sounds fascinating," he said. "I need tips on how to decorate my fishing cabin."

"I'd like to see it." Her eyes shone. "You probably need curtains. A nice rug to soften the ruggedness of the place."

"The only thing I want soft there, is you. I'd like to keep you there, naked." He crowded her space, enjoying how a tremor rippled through her body.

"Would you tie me up?"

"Baby, this is a path you don't want to go down," He took a piece of her hair, tugged on it slightly.

Simone pressed herself against his chest, wrapping her arms around his neck. "I think I do."

Dammit. Another time. If they had met before, he would have jumped in with both feet. But not now, when he'd had this wound that would never heal. When he'd had this wound that would never heal, he would have jumped in with both feet.

Quinn took her hands from around his neck with a groan, kissing her hard, his tongue circling hers.

"I know some people who can find out where those text messages are coming from. Come see them with me?"

"Okay."

He kissed the back of her knuckles. "More of this later?"

The heat in her eyes answered him, and he cursed himself. The wise thing to do would be to stop this before it went further, but he needed her close.

"Yes."

"Dinner tonight." Quinn traced her lips. "Pick the place."

"I know a great restaurant near me."

"Text me." His lips softly glided over hers, her vanilla and peach scent engulfing him.

8

CHAPTER EIGHT

"How was breakfast?" Quinn asked Harper at her desk in the executive wing of Axis Management.

"Breakfast was fine. Morning, Simone, it's nice to see you again," Harper said.

"Thanks." Simone blushed.

Quinn took her hand in his and smiled at her.

Harper furiously typed on her keyboard, clicked a button on her headset, and gestured. "They're in Xander's office."

"He should give you more time off," Quinn said.

"You try telling him that." Harper smiled.

"He doesn't deserve you." Quinn rapped his knuckles on her desk and Harper laughed.

"Are all of you friends here?" Simone asked.

"In this division, yes. Most of us have known each other for years. Some of us served in the military together. This way."

He rapped on the door opened it to what is known as the "black forest." The entire office suite, from the gorgeous black wooden floors to the black curtains parted to the mountain view, was black.

"That's Xander Montague!"

Quinn's lips twitched. Xander, the mysterious billionaire, had that effect on people. The co-CEO of Axis Security Management lounged with his feet up on the desk, looking at three monitors. With his long black hair, painted black fingernails, he looked like a Goth kid grown up. Xander had the shrewdest mind Quinn knew, and he was fiercely loyal, which was why he and Quinn got along. Also why, Quinn could crash in his new digs, despite his fist putting a hole through his office wall only last week, after Xander tried to cajole him to see the shrink.

He didn't need anyone telling him he had problems. He used not seeing the shrink as an excuse to sit out on Team Stealth. Yeah, he was a pussy.

"Got the hole patched, huh?" Quinn said.

"Asshole," Xander shot back. He unfolded his six-foot-five frame and extended his hand to Simone.

"Xander Montague. You did some work for a buddy of mine, Clive O'Neil."

"Yes! His main floor was an experiment. It worked out perfectly." Simone's eyes glowed. "It's all white, except orange pieces in different shades. Orange sofas, orange coffee table, orange pillow—"

"I get the picture." Quinn couldn't help smiling at her. Seeing Simone animated, talking about her passion tugged at him.

Seeing Simone lit up and animated made Quinn happy.

"That place was actually an inspiration for Meredith's wedding. Didn't it look gorgeous?"

"It did," Quinn agreed. "The entire room and decorations were white, and the bride wore red."

Xander raised his eyebrow. "Black, my bride, would wear black, and the only colour would be violet."

"She thinks the suite needs paintings."

Xander raised an eyebrow. "I know just the artist."

The door opened to admit the other Montague brother. Ares grinned and nodded from across the room.

Where Xander stood behind the scenes, Ares was the public face.

"Hey, there's trouble," Ares said, giving Quinn a brotherly hug. "Glad to hear you postponed the fishing trip."

Quinn shrugged. "Something came up."

"I can see that." The other man focused on Simone, taking her hand in his. "Ares Montague, nice to meet you." With his curly blond hair and angelic good looks, Ares caught a lot of women off guard.

Simone blushed as Ares kissed her hand.

"What brings you in this morning?" Xander asked, meeting Quinn's gaze.

"Someone has been sending threatening text messages to Simone," he said quietly. "Wondered if you could help find the source."

"Sorry to hear that," Ares said. "I'm sure we can help—"

"HELLO!" A shrill female voice pierced the air. "Did you miss me?"

Quinn closed his eyes. Kayleigh was here.

His purple-haired sister appeared in the doorway, wearing a short skirt, billowy blouse, fishnets, and funky green glasses. Quinn frowned. He worried that one day, her deep thirst for attention was going to get her in trouble.

"You can't barge in here," Quinn said.

"I didn't barge" Kayleigh answered airily. "Harper waved me in. I'm family. Don't you ever answer your phone?"

"I did," Quinn told her, keeping his voice calm and even. "You didn't answer yours, but I waited two hours for you."

Kayleigh waved her hand at him. "I got caught up." She glanced at Simone then did a double take. "Oh my God! You're Simone Roberts! Can I interview you for my podcast? It's just for a small indie publication, but I would love to have you on the show."

"I'd like that," Simone said.

"This is a lot, I know." Quinn squeezed her hand.

"It's fine." Simone squeezed back.

"She's with you?" Kayleigh's eyes went wide. "I can't wait to tell Fiona."

"Kayleigh," Quinn said in a warning tone.

"Okay. I'll keep it hushed." His sister pouted.

"We need Quinn for a few minutes, and we'll look over your phone, Simone," Xander raised his eyebrow. Quinn knew he was trying to soften his expression but it made him look more forbearing. "Need your phone again," Quinn said. He held out his hand and Simone smiled.

"This is becoming a habit." She glowed when she smiled. He couldn't resist her kind of trusting innocence. But he would do everything he could to stop whoever was taking advantage of her, whoever it was that wanted to hurt her.

"Can you ladies entertain yourselves?" Ares asked, holding the door open for them.

"Oh, that won't be a problem." Kayleigh slung her arm over Simone's shoulders and took her over to Harper's desk.

Quinn gritted his teeth. He didn't trust his sister not to talk Simone's ear off, but there wasn't anything he could do about it. He closed the door and faced these two powerful men he had trusted.

"Give it to us. Some dude walks into a restaurant you happen to be at and...?" Xander asked.

"Calls me the 'fire guy.' I thought he was on drugs or out of his mind until fifty thousand landed in my account. He said to make sure Simone was in the house when the fire was set."

"Fuckin bastard," Ares said.

"Yeah, but I don't know who the fucker is yet. I tracked Simone down and found her at Meredith Phillips's wedding. She has a segment on the breakfast show that everyone seems to have seen except me. Her ex-husband also had a business. From the sounds of it, people aren't happy he left."

"Do you remember anything about the guy who gave you money?" Xander crossed his arms over his chest and leaned against the front of his desk.

"Disguised in big clothes and—I think—a wig. I tried to catch a picture of his ride, but the dude wandered off towards the highway."

"Did you think of telling her she's in danger?" Xander asked, tilting his head.

"No." Quinn glared at the brothers.

"She's that special to make you go rogue?" Xander pressed.

"I can handle this," Quinn snapped. "You can back me up or not, but I'm going to keep her safe."

"Why?" Xander asked.

He didn't want to tell them his reasons, and he knew Xander could guess. It went beyond his need to keep a vulnerable woman safe. It might be about proving he could still do this, but he would not admit that.

"Because I can. Good enough?"

"If you told her and we took her on as a client, we could offer her more. Give me her phone."

"If I tell her, she's going to get spooked. Let me handle this my way." Quinn passed the phone to Xander.

His boss ran a cable through it, tapped furiously on his keyboard. "Going to send this to Nick because our tech department is swamped right now."

Axis Management kept their teams small, and the Cyber Unit was busy tracking down who was behind the attack last June.

"Going to talk about it?" Xander's steel eyes glared at him.

"Nothing to talk about."

"Why are you acting like such a scaredy cat and won't go see Dr. Laktur?"

"You know how my mom is." He cursed himself for using Deirdre as an excuse, but he needed Xander off his back.

"You got shrink clearance when you were with CISIS. What's the difference?"

"I'm fine. It's time for me to do something different."

"Hey man, I want you on the payroll permanently. We need someone training the next batch of operatives over the winter."

The truth was, he'd quit—told them he wasn't going to go any more jobs with Team Stealth—because he couldn't imagine working with them again.

"Hey, Quinn, I need to talk to you about that thing," Kayleigh said, opening the door.

"Later." Automatically, he steeled himself for Kayleigh's tantrum, but his sister nodded and leaned against the door. Simone's phone rang.

"She can answer. I copied all the data and sent it to Nick."

"Simone, come get your phone," Kayleigh called.

Her smile soothed his angsty vibes. Her peachy scent as she passed him calmed him. Damn this woman was doing things to him he wasn't prepared for.

"Hi, Marion."

Wincing, Simone put the phone away from her face.

"Okay. What did Carson do? Calm down. I can do that. No, it's not a problem." Simone closed her phone.

"That sounded intense," Ares commented.

"My mother-in-law is a real estate agent, and her assistant, Carson, mixed up her schedule. Clients are at the house, and they can't open the lockbox. She can't get anyone else to come, and the lockbox isn't opening for them. I've got to go."

"Marion Boucher?" Xander asked.

"Yes," Simone said, that rosy blush spreading across her cheeks. Quinn bit his lip to keep from smiling.

Ares let out a low whistle. "Your mother-in-law has sold half the city."

"Yeah, she's good at what she does," Simone said.

"I can drive you." Quinn wanted her close by.

"I'll take an Uber," Simone said, shaking her head. "It's on the other side of the city,"

"I'm going that way," Kayleigh offered.

He didn't like it, but it'd make him look like a control freak if he said anything.

"Hey, why don't we take the limo?" Ares asked. "I have to see a client, anyway."

"Sounds good!" Kayleigh said.

"See you tonight?" Quinn brushed her arm.

"Can't wait."

She gave him a little wave and followed Ares and Kayleigh out of the office.

"You're so screwed," Xander said, slapping a hand on his back. "You have it bad for this woman,"

"Don't call my mom for a painting."

"I don't take orders."

His boss stared him down. Quinn stood toe-to-toe with him. It was illogical, to blame him for Jordan's death. He couldn't help it. That mission had been a clusterfuck.

"Could Marion have pissed someone off and they're after Simone?" Quinn asked.

"She's been known to cause a scene," Xander said. "And a couple of deals haven't gone her way lately."

"I'll look into it. Going to track down Simone's ex," Quinn said, stepping to the door. He found it hard being in the same space as Xander for more than a few minutes and needed to leave.

"Let us know if you need anything," Xander said.

"Later."

9

CHAPTER NINE

T he latest events in her life had turned from a fantasy into a fairy-tale. Simone flushed as Ares smiled at her. This morning, she'd expected to be having pancakes with the bridesmaids at the hotel, not in a limo with someone from the headlines. Doing what Quinn said, she texted Mielle to say she was all right. Simone smiled, reading the answering text that Ava was still crashed out.

"How did you meet Quinn? I'm so happy to see him with someone. His last girl was a slag," Kayleigh said.

"Kayleigh, that's an awful word." Ares nudged Quinn's sister with his foot.

"What? She wasn't very nice to my brother—or me. How come you didn't tell me he was going out again?"

"I only met Simone minutes before you did."

Kayleigh stuck her tongue out at Ares, revealing a piercing, then turned her full attention to Simone.

"You know, we can't pay you for the interview. I should have mentioned it. Ares, why don't you buy a media company, and I'll be a writer there?"

Ares spread his hands wide and gave Simone a conspiratorial wink. "I know nothing about running a media company."

"It's okay," Simone said, smiling. "The studio is always after me to do more interviews and appearances. You'll be giving me good PR."

When Kayleigh smiled or made a gesture, she did it with her complete self. Her entire face lit up, and she frequently clapped her hands; Simone immediately liked her.

The girl was friendly and easy to be around, almost constantly chattering. "So, when was it you met Quinn at the club? I can't believe you guys didn't tell me. If you would let me go, I would know!"

"I don't go," Ares said.

Kayleigh waved at him and clutched Simone's arm. "He doesn't, that's true. He and Xander are too private for that."

Kayleigh's exuberance helped settle her nerves. Simone wondered about their relationship. She longed for that kind of friendship evident between them. She loved Ava and Meredith, but they weren't close in this familiar way of Kayleigh and Ares.

"I haven't been to the club either. I met Quinn at my friend Meredith's wedding."

The limo bumped over a pothole. Kayleigh squeaked and clutched Simone's arm harder.

"Meredith Phillips! You're so lucky! Is she as nice as she seems? You can never tell with some people." Kayleigh nodded at Ares.

"She's a good friend of mine, and yes, she is nice," Simone said.

"Wow. I can't believe Quinn went to a wedding. That's progress, right?"

Ares inclined his head. "You can take it as a positive sign."

"Good. I thought I had lost him, and losing two brothers would suck. Where's this house you are going to?"

Two brothers? Quinn had only mentioned Kayleigh. Simone put it out of her mind for now and brought up a photo of the house.

"Wow! Ares, buy that house for me!"

"It's all the way out in the middle of nowhere, and you don't drive."

Kayleigh shrugged. "I can't wait to tell Mom. She's packing up some paintings to ship to the gallery, but I bet I can catch her—"

"Don't tell your mother, Kayleigh. You know how private Quinn is," Ares said.

"Yes, okay. I'm just happy for him. And you. Are you sure you like him?"

For a moment, Kayleigh's effervescence vanished, and Simone saw an open and vulnerable expression, fear of rejection clear on her face

"Yes. I like him," she said quietly.

She didn't have the heart to tell Kayleigh it was just a—she didn't know what it was. Last night, she'd thought it was a one-night stand. But one night had turned into two. What did that make it? A fling, Simone decided.

"Good. He's overprotective, but he is fiercely loyal, right, Ares? Oh, my God, you're on your phone again."

"Quinn mentioned that your mother paints. What kind of painting?" Simone asked, drawing Kayleigh's attention.

"Usually, it's an abstract piece that is a social commentary. Here." Kayleigh passed her phone over to Simone.

Simone flipped through the pieces on the National Gallery page.

"I wasn't expecting this," Simone said, stunned to read the name. Many of her clients would love a piece by Deirdre Snow.

"Yeah, she's rad. I kind of wonder what kind of artist she would be if she wasn't bipolar, but she's made it work to her advantage."

"Oh, Kayleigh, we need a ball gag for you," Ares said with a half-hearted chuckle.

Simone shifted in the leather seat. "That must be hard."

Kayleigh squeezed her hand and nodded.

As the car stopped at the big, white blocky house, Simone's mind whirred. So Quinn had left out some details. So he hadn't shared his entire life story. They had just met, after all.

Her swirling thoughts came to an abrupt halt when she glanced out the window. On the porch, with their arms crossed, their expressions identically stony, stood the power couple.

"They do not look happy." Simone's stomach tightened. She hated conflict.

"Kayleigh, stay here," Ares said.

"Fine. I'll text you the details of the interview. Nice meeting you!" Kayleigh called.

Ares offered Simone his hand and leaned into her ear. "What is their name?"

"Winston-Cartwright."

"Mr. and Mrs. Winston-Cartwright, I want to apologize for keeping you waiting. I had to borrow Simone, Marion's talented daughter-in-law, and it is completely my fault she let you wait. Please accept my apologies."

"Ah... It's all right," Mr. Winston-Cartwright stammered. Simone smiled at his reaction to Ares Montague on his potential future lawn.

"It was last minute," chimed in his wife.

"Simone, call me if you need a lift." Ares kissed her cheek, turned and waved at them before disappearing into the limo.

"Hello! I'm so happy to show this house to you. I know you are going to love it." Simone smiled, punched in the code, and opened the doors for the Winston-Cartwrights.

The scent of rotten food assaulted her, causing bile to rise in her throat. It took a moment for her brain to process the unexpected mess, and it crashed into her cloud of euphoria and brought her back down to earth.

"Sorry, sorry, there is electrical wiring all over. I'm afraid we can't go in." She slapped the doors.

Mrs. Winston-Cartwright frowned and peered at Simone over her sunglasses.

"But we're here now, and we already waited for you! Let us in. We won't step on anything."

"I'm sorry, but I have to get an electrician out. We have to be safe, for insurance reasons. I can show you the gardens and the pool at the back."

In the Uber on the way home, it took Simone six tries to get through to Marion.

"You're a dear for showing the house. If they buy it, I'll give you the commission. Can you believe the hair salon isn't open at six a.m.? What are we early risers supposed to do?"

"Eat breakfast?" Simone rolled her eyes.

"I guess, but then I have to go into the dining room or restaurant, and people will see me with my hair like this. I must have gotten too much sun."

"Marion, there's something wrong with the house."

"Did they complain about the price? In this market, I could have raised it by another seventy thousand, but it's been sitting there for a while."

"No, it's not the asking price, it's—"

"Oh, they don't like the double garage? I'm not a fan of the design myself, but they could knock it down or make it into something else. It just takes a little creativity; maybe you can give them suggestions, Simone."

"No, Marion, they didn't comment on the garage."

"Then it's the pool, isn't it? I know it's not—"

"MARION!" Simone yelled so loudly her Uber driver looked back at her. Simone waved an apology and lowered her voice.

"Someone trashed the house. Garbage and rotten food were all over the hallway. It looks like paint or something was thrown on the furniture, and there are holes in the walls. That's all I saw from the doorway. I didn't let the Winston-Cartwrights in."

For all her bluster, her mother-in-law cared about her business, and Simone wished she could see her face.

"Oh," Marion almost whispered after a moment. "Simone, could you hire a professional cleaning company for me and tell them to take lots of pictures before they start? I want to use someone I don't normally go to."

"Marion, I think you need to call the police."

"Simone, please can you call the cleaning company?"

"Okay," Simone said. "It doesn't bother you?"

"Yes. But this is how I want to handle it."

"Okay, Marion." Simone didn't want to push her mother-in-law; Marion had done so much for her.

"Thank you, Simone."

Before the Uber dropped her off, Simone had arranged for a cleaning company.

After changing her clothes, she took a sketchbook and show notes and settled into her favourite corner of the garden, on her comfy lounger chair. The garden was her favourite part of the house and the reason she hadn't moved.

She only used the downstairs, which included a small studio at the back, where she met with clients because she really didn't need this much house.

Simone titled her face to the afternoon sun and opened a blank page in her sketchbook.

She sketched the tall purple phlox creeping up her lattice, but her mind kept wandering to Quinn. Before she knew it, the lines on her page formed a strong jawline. Another few lines, the outline of the face of the strange man who'd whisked her away, appeared on the page.

Who'd whisked her away and had sex with her. Her mind drifted to being against the cold metal of the washing machine.

A part of her wanted Quinn to invite her over to do his laundry again.

Another part of her wondered how she had stepped out of her perfectly predictable life and into the life of someone who went home with strangers. Someone who let strange men spank her. No, not a stranger, Quinn.

Quinn gave her orgasms, tied her up, and spanked her. To her surprise, the spanking hadn't hurt, not exactly. At first, there was heat, and it stung where his hand landed, but a moment later, a pleasant warmth infused her body beginning from the site of the sting.

Squirming in the lounger, she remembered how pliable she had become under Quinn's voice and hands, how much she wanted to please him. In submitting, her brain turned off, lost the sensations. She liked his appreciation of her. He made her feel like he could handle anything with those big shoulders of his. A shudder rippled through her as she remembered the feel of his hands sliding down her back, his expression when she did what he asked. She closed her sketchbook on the half-finished drawing and stretched out on the lounger.

She wanted to have sex with Quinn, and she hoped the night ended with him seeing her bedroom. Grabbing her tablet, she ran a search on dominance and submission. Most of what came up she had come across before. Some images made her ache between her legs.

Sliding a hand under the waistband of her panties, Simone closed her eyes. Her other hand went to her nipples, remembering how Quinn had manipulated them. She pinched her nipple hard, and wetness soaked her fingers between her legs. She circled her clit, moving her fingers back and forth, remembering the feel of Quinn's fiery breath on her pussy.

Her toes curled as she threw her head back, the orgasm sweeping over her. She pulled the blanket around her, smiling as she remembered Quinn's command to keep her eyes open as he brought her to climax.

She woke to her neighbour's German shepherd barking up a storm. "Easy Fox, it's just a critter in the bushes." Thankful for the interruption, Simone gathered her stuff. She couldn't wait for her date.

10

CHAPTER TEN

Quinn thumped the steering wheel in frustration. All these hours later and not any closer to finding out who had hired him. The whole thing screamed amateur. The guy didn't ask for a code word, had no way to verify if Quinn was the person they had arranged to meet at the restaurant. The only thing that made him take it as a genuine threat was the fifty thousand dollars in his account.

Quinn pulled up the search results on Simone's ex-husband while he waited for her in front of the Colombian restaurant, tucked out of the way in a strip mall.

Liam Boucher had dropped off the planet as much as possible. He didn't have any social media under his name, but through a charity that rebuilt homes in disaster-struck areas, he found a picture of Liam next to the director of the charity, with a hammer in his hand.

Quinn snorted. Maybe he should have run off to Peru. His dad had taught him to swing a hammer.

He'd crafted an image of Liam in his mind as someone being small and geeky, but the mineralogist had well-defined muscles, a smile that said he could be trusted, and clear hazel eyes. Quinn wanted to punch the guy. He sent Logan, who occasionally volunteered with disaster relief charities, the info he had discovered, asking him to validate his findings, but he didn't think it likely Liam was behind the threat against Simone.

Catching sight of Simone, walking into the restaurant's parking lot, in the review mirror, he got out of the truck and jogged over to her. "I would have been happy to pick you up."

She didn't know someone had arranged to kill her, but those texts should have been enough to make her take caution. Quinn's nostrils flared as he put an arm around Simone.

"It's only a fifteen-minute walk. I wanted to clear my thoughts."

The scent of vanilla and peach wafted through his nostrils. He leaned in and nuzzled her ear.

"What thoughts were you trying to clear away?" He moved in and pressed his mouth to hers, hard and fast, those pink berry lips too damn kissable to ignore.

Her soft sighs against him fired sparks in his brain. And he should stop this before it went any further. But she felt so right. So good.

Quinn pulled his mouth from hers, rubbed his thumb along her jawline.

"Trying to process what we did this morning, last night."

Quinn leaned into her ear. "It's all I can think about too."

The image of the sunlight casting her in golden hues to match her hair went through his mind, and he wondered what it would be like to wake up beside her every morning. He shook his head.

What he had with Simone only extended to keeping her safe. A temporary arrangement, not a long-term one. In two days, he would be on his way to his fishing cabin, back home. His stomach tightened at the thought and he pushed the feeling of slight dread away and nuzzled Simone's ear.

"You seemed to like it." He put his hand on the small of her back and guided her into the restaurant.

"Yes, I did, but I don't know why I did or should."

"Because it's fun and hot, it gets you out of your head," Quinn said.

He would never tire of seeing that pink blush spread against her fair cheeks. "It felt like—"

With a tug on her waist, he brought her right beside him. "Felt like what?"

"Scary. Good. I didn't have to think about what to do. I wanted to please you, and that scared me."

"Wanting to please me is scary?"

Her cheeks dimpled slightly as she smiled and ducked her head. "Yes."

He took her chin in his hand, rubbed his thumb on her bottom lip, and kissed her behind her ear. "Good. Let's eat."

As the rain fell harder, they got into the restaurant just in the nick of time.

The restaurant's red and gold plaster walls, with the low lighting and intimate booths, gave it a warm and cozy feel. "This place looks great."

"It's my favourite," Simone said. "I got sick of waiting for Liam to come home, so every night, I walked the neighbourhood and found this place."

She was sharing her favourite spot with him, and damn if that didn't make him feel all warm inside.

A friendly server sat them in a booth and took their drink orders.

Quinn slid in right next to Simone and continued the conversation. "He was absent a lot?"

"Yes, work pressure got to him. He took off and escaped. Sometimes he would just leave. We would have dinner, he would get up and walk out, or I would find him gone when I got out of the shower, until one day he just left and didn't come back."

Yeah, her ex was an asshole but not a killer. Quinn shrugged. "His loss."

The look of surprise in her eyes made him want to plow her ex-husband through a wall.

"I wish I had ended the marriage sooner. I knew it wasn't working. But I wanted to make my dad happy."

Quinn couldn't imagine making a life choice because a parent of his asked him to; then again, his parents weren't award-worthy.

"You have a big heart."

Blushing, Simone shook her head.

The server dropped off their drinks—red wine for her and an iced tea for him—and took their orders, then briskly scurried towards the kitchen.

"Tell me about what you're processing."

He took her hand in his, rubbing his thumb along her index finger, then slid one foot between hers and nudged her closer to him.

"Reading about dominance and submission, and how people live like this. Was this always a thing for you?"

"Was what a thing for me?" He wanted her to speak plainly and voice her thoughts.

She didn't meet his eyes, distracted herself by fidgeting with the silverware. After a moment, she shook her head.

He put a hand on her neck and felt her shiver slightly.

"Wanting to dominate a woman?"

"Yes," Quinn stroked her hair. "I always wanted to tie girls up and spank them. I always wanted to be in charge. It wasn't until the summer before I enlisted, I found out other people did it too and learned about kink and D/s."

"That's young," Simone said.

"I met someone who kind of mentored me."

He smiled warily, remembering Max, Jordan's uncle who had caught him rifling through his porn collection.

Jordan had wondered why he'd spent so much time with Max that summer, and years later, when he found out, he'd laughed and said he always knew his uncle was a kinky bastard. Max took away the porn, gave him stacks of books to read about the ins and outs of D/s, and when Quinn reached the age of majority, took him to his first BDSM club.

"How come you didn't ask me to call you 'sir'?" Simone's soft question drew him out of his memories.

Quinn took her hands in his, enjoying how she leaned forward, eager to hear what he had to say.

"Honorifics can help put one in the mindset of submission, but for me, hearing my name as a woman screams out an orgasm, or asking me by name to give her a spanking, is more intimate than an honorific."

Those words sounded good, and Quinn thought even she might believe them, but he knew it for bullshit. If Simone called him "sir," that would imply another level. A committed level he didn't want to be at.

"There are no rules, then?" Simone said. "It's all preference?"

"The cornerstone of a D/s relationship is trust, and it is safe, sane, and consensual, but the day-to-day living is as varied as any vanilla relationship. If I were to have a full-time sub, we would have rules and consequences for breaking those rules."

"But you cooked for me and made me coffee."

"And you did my laundry," Quinn said. He placed his thumb and index finger under her chin until her gaze met his. "I don't want a servant. If I were to have a long-term relationship, I would want someone who trusts me enough to put themselves in my hands, who sees that I can care for them, who lets me care for them, and is honest enough, vulnerable enough to tell me what they need. I want someone who will let me push them where they think their trust is, to trust me even further."

Her eyes widened, and a deep rose flush crept up her neck. "How does that work?"

Damn, he couldn't believe she'd asked. He wrapped a strand of her hair around his finger. "Take off your panties and hand them to me."

Her eyes grew big. Quinn smiled as her breath became shallow.

"You're serious?"

"Yes." He put as much command in his voice as he could and noticed a shiver rake through her.

He wanted a female's submission because the sub found it as much fulfillment in submission as he did in dominance.

She turned her head from side to side and, seeing that familiar blush spread across her cheeks, Quinn squeezed her arm.

"What's stopping you?"

"I have nylons on. I would have to kick my shoes off and take my nylons off."

He ran a finger lightly over her earlobe, smiling at her slight shiver.

"You've taken off heels and nylons lots of times. What's different about this?"

"We're in a restaurant. I don't want people to see me do it."

"Do you trust me?"

"Yes."

God, she shouldn't. She should run out of here right now. With her, he felt like joining life again. He was too selfish to leave; he couldn't.

"Then trust I got you. No one is watching, and I wouldn't jeopardize your safety." He chewed his lip to keep from smiling at the irony. She didn't know he had set out to protect her from the danger she was in. He wouldn't risk an indecent exposure charge.

She reached under the table, and his skin pulsed as he felt her hand against his leg.

"Okay."

He stretched a leg out and nudged her heel off her foot, then the other one.

In another moment, she put a silky bundle in his hands. Damn her response, her daring went straight to his head. He grinned at her.

"That's how it works. Good girl." He claimed her soft lips. The taste of her sparked his desire, and his cock stirred with need.

"I liked that, you telling me to do something I would never have thought to do because you wanted me to do it. If I hadn't done that, would you have punished me?"

He narrowed his eyes at her, noticing how she squirmed on the chair.

Discreetly, he put her panties in his inside jacket pocket.

"Yes. I would expect obedience. If you broke a rule, we would talk about it, and then I would punish you. If it happened again, it would be disrespectful, and it would tell me you weren't interested in this relationship. Remember, your submission is given freely. I'm not interested in taking it inch by inch."

He touched her cheek in reassurance.

"What would an example of your expectations be?"

"Other than being in control in the bedroom, I would expect the courtesy of you answering my calls as soon as you can. Ask for help when you need it, things like that."

Quinn watched as she looked down at her hands. Was she wondering if she could give him all this?

He lifted her chin with his finger and kissed her again; he wanted to claim her, to push her. He wanted to take this to a place he shouldn't. His tongue swirled around hers, her cheeks flushed, her breathing increased.

A polite cough made Quinn break off the kiss as the server put their food in front of them. He put his hand on her inner thigh, enjoying the rosy blush that spread across her face.

"Why is answering your call important to you?"

"For me, it's basic respect. I don't expect you to drop everything, but getting back to me as soon as you can is important to me. I've had people in my life I have had to worry about."

"I think I'm getting it," Simone said around a forkful of food. "The whole D/s thing."

"You are a natural submissive," Quinn said. He wanted to take her to Club Bandit and show her off and further her education. "I could watch you eat all day."

"Their food is so good." Simone smiled. "But you don't want a full-time relationship?"

Quinn shifted in his chair. The question felt like cold water being dumped over his head.

"I would rather have fun, and everyone involved knows what it is from the start. That's what I love about D/s. Everything is communicated and agreed to beforehand."

"I'm not ready for anything more than that, either."

The tightness in his chest eased a fraction.

"You told me your mother paints."

And with that simple comment, the food in his mouth tasted like sawdust. He sipped his iced tea and raised an eyebrow.

"Yes, she does."

"Kayleigh showed me her work on the National Gallery page. You didn't tell me your mother is Deirdre Snow. What's it like having an artist, a famous, well-known artist, as a mother?"

"It was okay." *Damn, you're being a coward.*

He wanted her to trust him. He couldn't ask her to be open and vulnerable to him without giving the same to her.

"When Deirdre was stable, it was fun. We got to make messes and tag along to gallery openings. We got to stay up late while she painted till the sun rose."

"I would have loved that. My father wouldn't let me go to art school. He agreed to Interior Design because an architect friend told him he used them all the time. I begged both my parents for art lessons."

Simone couldn't relate to how he'd grown up. Or understand it.

He thought of Jordan. His best friend had always said he made too much of his mother's illness.

"When she was off her meds or having an episode, it sucked." He swallowed, grateful for the interruption of the server clearing away plates.

When he looked at her, the compassion in her big brown eyes caught him off guard.

"That must have been so hard."

A lump formed in his throat. Quinn nodded. "Yeah. She was off her meds often because Deidre always thought she knew better than the doctors. She refused medication for years, trying alternative treatments ranging from colloidal silver to fish oil."

Simone squeezed his hand. "That sounds so hard."

Quinn exhaled. "Yeah. She's always put her art above her health and the way she's handled her illness caused a rift between us. I don't talk to her often."

"When was the last time you saw her?"

"Four months ago."

At Jordan's funeral. He hadn't been in the mood for Deirdre's drama.

The buzzing phone in his pocket saved him from telling her about that trip home. "I need to take this," Quinn said

"Of course."

Quinn reluctantly left the table, found a quiet corner by the bathroom.

"You got news, Nick?"

"That number that has been sending Simone texts goes back to JayJay Harris," Nick said.

Quinn frowned. "Doesn't ring a bell."

"Works as an admin assistant for an attorney's office downtown," Nick said.

"That doesn't seem to fit." So he still didn't have any answers about who had paid him to set Simone on fire. "Thanks, man. I owe you."

As he joined Simone back at their table, how much he lusted for her made him lose his breath. With the light hitting her hair just so, she looked so pretty. Quinn knew he didn't deserve her.

"The trace on your phone came back. Do you know anyone by the name of JayJay Harris?"

She shook her head. "No, it's not familiar."

"What was happening when you first got these text messages?"

"It was right after I got the spot on the show."

"You didn't think it was from a fan?"

"No. My fans are mostly women, and I can't see them doing this, not that women can't be violent. But it's only text messages."

"In my experience, text messages escalate."

"Your work is good at keeping people safe." Simone fidgeted with the tablecloth. "Do you have plans for Monday?"

He felt annoyed that she changed the subject and could guess she didn't like confrontation. He would work on that with her, showing her that he wanted every emotion that ran through that golden-hued head of hers.

"I'm heading to my fishing cabin on Monday."

"Oh." Her tone was heavy with disappointment.

"It's more than a fishing trip. I have to stop to visit my childhood home and say goodbye to a friend." A lump formed in his throat. He wasn't looking forward to that trip. To say goodbye to the house that had been a second home to him. "Want to get out of here?"

In reply, she put down her glass and took his hand.

He paid their tab, slung his arm around her shoulders, and led her outside. He opened the passenger door for her, went around, and let himself in.

"Give me directions."

He knew where she lived, but he didn't want to appear like a stalker. A short drive later, he pulled into her driveway.

"That's quite a house."

"Not what I want. Marion let me keep it. She said there was no sense in moving out because it wasn't my choice." The emotion in her voice took him by surprise.

He cupped the back of her neck. "Are you alright?"

Simone sniffed, clearly holding back tears.

"When I said yes to you last night, it made me realize how little I have chosen. I married Liam because my father wanted to see me married. I live in this house because it was easier than finding somewhere on my own. I became an interior designer because my father thought it more acceptable than being an artist. I wanted to go to art school."

The determination in her voice took Quinn back.

"It's your life, and no one is telling you what to do now."

"Except you."

"Only with your consent." Quinn traced her lips lightly.

He leaned forward, his tongue eagerly probing the feel of her mouth, sent tremors through his body, making his cock like stone.

"Can we go inside?" He ripped his mouth away from hers with an effort.

"Yes."

The heavy rain jumped back up off the pavement, and the wind nearly ripped off the truck's door.

"I want you so bad. I can't wait until you are under me. Hold on."

Simone yelped and laughed as he scooped her up.

"That's better," Quinn said.

He kissed her, and the sweet taste of her flooded his system. He needed her now. She responded to his kiss, opening her mouth for him. Her fingers dug into his shoulders, his tongue dominated hers, and she pressed herself against him. Damn, this woman was undoing him.

The shattering of glass caused adrenaline to surge in his veins. The next moment, he covered her body with his on the cool pavement. Rain pelted his back.

He waited a moment more, listened for other sounds, then got up, feeling the glass in his arms underneath his feet. Underneath him, Simone trembled, her eyes wide. "Quinn, my windshield."

Holding her hand, Quinn peered into the shattered windshield. On the front seat was a brick with a piece of paper wrapped around it. The bold words scrawled in black read, "Die bitch."

"I can't believe—" Simone sobbed.

He held her against his chest while looking around, listening for footsteps or for a car driving away. Hardly a sound in her quiet, upscale neighbourhood.

"Simone, give me your keys," Quinn said.

Simone fished them out of her purse and put them in his hand. Making sure there was no glass, Quinn opened the driver's side door, and put the keys on the seat.

"Why did you do that?"

"I'm going to get someone to look after your car. I want it inspected in case it's more than a brick."

Simone's face paled. Quinn cursed. He couldn't help but be direct.

"Come on." He helped a trembling Simone over to his truck.

He barely buckled up before racing out of her driveway. "I've got you."

Hitting the voice command, he called Xander.

"Yes?"

"A brick sailed for Simone's head moments ago. Landed through her car window instead. Keys are on the driver's seat. Can you get someone to check it out?"

"Of course. You're on the way to the suite?"

"Yes," Quinn said.

"Erik is a minute away on another job."

"No. I'll circle back myself," Quinn said, through gritted teeth.

"I'm sending him in. If whoever threw the brick is watching her place, he'll find them."

"Thought he was off rotation." Quinn gritted his teeth. He hated hearing the name responsible for Jordan's death.

"We're short-staffed. You take care of Simone. We'll take care of the scene."

He didn't like it, but he had to care for Simone, not fight over his backup's operation.

"You think they meant it for my head?" she whispered.

He cursed. So much for not scaring her.

"I think the timing was suspicious."

He sped to Axis Management and, moments later, rushed her into the suite.

"Can you hold me?"

And with her ask, his heart rate slowed. He noticed the cut on her collarbone and shards of glass that dotted her skin and hair.

"Yes."

He could hold her. He would rather her be in handcuffs to keep her safe, but holding her was what she needed right now.

11
CHAPTER ELEVEN

Simone tried to relax in Quinn's embrace, but her body trembled against him. The sound of glass breaking reverberated through her mind, and she couldn't stop shaking.

"I've got you." Quinn took her by the arm.

Every time he said that to her, she believed him.

She stumbled, and he caught her, guiding her to the kitchen.

Her fingers touched her hairline and came away sticky with blood. Her stomach churned.

"Right over here, I'll clean you up."

Quinn gently took her hand, put it under the faucet, and ran lukewarm water over it. Then he lifted her to the counter. He slid her jacket from her shoulders and caressed the side of her cheek.

Her hands shook as she tried to steady herself.

She should have taken these messages seriously, but she didn't understand why someone would want to hurt her. In her experience, people always blew security threats out of proportion.

"What are you thinking?"

She wrung her hands and focused on Quinn. "You were right. It escalated from text messages. It's related, isn't it?"

"Yes."

He passed her a bottle of water and opened a first aid kit. The kit had dented corners and shiny worn Power Puff and Kim Possible stickers on the sides.

"What do I do about it?" Simone asked.

"We'll figure it out."

Simone tried to shake off her nerves. "That's an impressive first aid kit. I like the stickers. From your Army days?"

The hard case first-aid kit had multiple slots for different bandages, a couple of different pills in bottles, ointment, sports tape, splints, and other looking medical things.

"I'm no medic. That's my friend, Gabe. And the stickers are from my sister, from when she was a kid. Let's get this glass out of your hair first." Quinn took out a pair of tweezers from his kit and motioned for her to turn her head. One by one he plucked the glass shards out of her hair and scalp and dropped them into an empty coffee mug.

She released a soft sigh when he stepped back.

"Now your face. Tip your face to the light, that's it." His warm hands were gentle and sure.

"Ow!" Simone said, as the tweezers grazed her skin.

"You didn't make this much noise when I spanked your ass" God, every time he smiled, it changed his face. Made the hard planes softer, his eyes lighter.

"It didn't hurt this much," Simone said.

"Then I went too light on you," Quinn smirked.

"It stings!"

"Take a deep breath," Quinn said. "Stop moving."

Breathing in through her nose, Simone picked a spot on the ceiling to stare at and tried to stay still.

"No, this kit is mine because I've needed it. When Deirdre had an episode, she often hurt herself. I learnt to patch her up, and my first aid skills improved over the years. Carrying the kit is a habit."

Holding still, Simone breathed through her nose and tried not to move. She saw him tense up his shoulders. The air between them grew from electric to intensely intimate.

"That sounds tough," Simone said, wanting to touch his arm, to offer him comfort, but she held still, hoping he would keep talking.

"Yep. One night, Deirdre climbed onto the roof, wanting to paint the stars. Getting down, she missed two steps on the ladder and ended up with a broken wrist. Having splints was useful."

Leaning forward, she put her hands on his big shoulders and rubbed circles on them, wanting to ease his pain.

"Didn't anyone help you?"

"It was the roof incident that brought our neighbour running. She'd moved in two months before and tried to make friends. We were terrified of someone calling the child protection services on us. Deirdre always said if they came to our door, she wouldn't be able to paint ever again. Her biggest fear is that her illness will stop her from painting."

Simone couldn't imagine. Her parents were busy and aloof, but they didn't need her to take care of them.

With an effort, she bit the inside of her cheek, holding still, hoping Quinn would continue.

"The neighbour was also impressed with my first aid kit. She was a nurse. Deirdre wouldn't let a stranger touch her, but Fiona guided me on how to set her wrist, and it was better than how I had splinted her ankle earlier that summer. Another neighbour had called the ambulance. They came, my dad came and went with her to the hospital, where they admitted her for another round of psych observation."

"What happened to you and Kayleigh and—"

She didn't know the other brother's name.

Quinn turned from her, washing his hands under the facet. He gathered the garbage and closed his kit, then rummaged in a drawer.

"Here, eat." He passed her a protein bar.

She took the bar, unwrapped it slowly, and ate a tiny piece of it.

"Gross," Simone said.

"You look cute when you eat gross food."

Simone scrunched up her nose at him, and he laughed. He sat beside her on the counter, his shoulders touching hers.

"Fiona took us home that night and kept us," Quinn said, his voice soft.

"What do you mean, she kept you?"

"From that night on, we stayed with her often, especially when Deirdre was having an episode. She made friends with my parents and tried to get Deirdre some help."

"What did your parents think about this?"

He gulped water and ran his hand through his hair. "I don't know. It helped my dad. I think it overwhelmed him, the stuff with Deirdre. He drank." His expression grew stony for a moment, then cleared. "As Fiona got through to Deirdre, my dad stayed around more, slowed down on the drinking. He got his carpentry business up off the ground."

"That's incredible," Simone said.

The shock in Quinn's blue eyes took her back. His powerful frame seemed to deflate.

"Not really."

She stared at him, his stormy expression, his hunched over shoulders, and she wrapped her arms around him, pressing her body into his.

"Your family needed help, and Fiona helped without making it worse. She sounds wonderful."

"She's the best. I thought—"

He jumped from the counter, strode over to the windows. Simone turned her head, watching him. God, every step he took had purpose. His well-honed muscles flexed as he crossed his arms, his back to her.

"I had been taking care of Kayleigh and Deirdre and living with her illness by myself for so long. I felt like I had failed."

"Oh, Quinn," Simone said.

"Yeah. I'm messed up."

"Your Dad couldn't handle it, and he was an adult. How old were you?"

"Eight."

Her cheeks felt wet, and she realized tears had been leaking out as she heard Quinn's story. "I'm glad Fiona was there," she said.

"You would like her. That night she became another mom to me."

"Sounds like you needed one."

"She's great. She's the friend I'm seeing on that fishing trip, it's a trip home to say goodbye. She's moving on. But I'm not ready to."

He turned, and the grief in his eyes made her uncomfortable, but she held herself still and met his eyes.

"Fiona also gave me the brother I didn't have before. Jordan," he said. "He was energetic and easy going, everyone loved him... and because I fucked up, I took him away from Fiona."

The pieces came together in her head. The lost brother. Not a blood relation, but a chosen one.

"That last job?"

"Yeah. Axis Management recruited Jordan when he was done with his last tour. He was the unlikeliest soldier, but you could count on him to always have your back. When Axis recruited him, he told them he wouldn't work for them without me."

His husky and hollow tone pulled at her heartstrings.

She slid off the stool, went to him with her arms open. In the next instance, he embraced her tight.

"Fuck. I shouldn't have told you all of that," Quinn said.

"No, it's okay," Simone said, she reached for him. His arms came around her.

"I'm supposed to be keeping *you* safe." His sensuous lips meet hers, sending a fresh wave of electric heat through her.

"You are," Simone said. "I feel safe being here with you."

At his intense glare, her stomach tightened in a bundle of nerves.

His cell rang, and he let go of her and grabbed it from the counter.

Her heart twisted for him as he paced back and forth. She wanted to ease his pain. Thinking back to what Kayleigh had told her on the limo ride, Simone understood him better. She could see how he loved with his complete self once someone got past those walls.

He'd let her in.

Going into the kitchen, Simone opened the fridge door, closed it again. She felt itchy and wanted to leave to get away from her feelings. Maybe she and Quinn had that in common. She had been taught to suck it up and do the proper thing, and he just didn't let anyone into his pain because he learnt to handle it all himself.

She knew, in that moment, she had fallen for this wounded man, and the thought sent a quaver of icy fear through her. He couldn't return her feelings. He'd made it clear to her he wouldn't.

Quinn ended his call, and his blue eyes zeroed in on her as if he knew her thoughts.

Simone swallowed. She wanted him to know how she felt about him, and she also wanted to run out the door. Quinn took her hands in his strong, callused ones. She exhaled. She was here for the moment, and she didn't want to be anywhere else.

"Xander said the police have been by and have chalked it up to a minor incident of vandalism. He told them you would be available for a statement tomorrow morning. He's had your car towed to the garage to get the windshield repaired and have it checked over by a mechanic. The garage will drop off your car to you, here, tomorrow morning. Unless you want to go home?"

She didn't want to go home to that empty house where an attacker had gotten to her; she didn't think she ever wanted to step foot in that house again.

"No." She shook her head.

As he looked at her with his observant gaze, he made her squirm. "Are you sure?"

"Yes. I'm sorry to involve you in this."

His finger on her lips shushed her. "You didn't. Coincidental timing."

She put her hands on his broad shoulders, and he kissed her, his lips soft. The clean, woodsy smell of him grew familiar, and she wanted to inhale it. His tongue met hers, and she opened to him, inviting him in.

He broke off the kiss. "How are you feeling?"

"I'm overwhelmed."

"It's not every day you get a brick thrown at you." He ran his hand through her hair.

Simone laughed. "Thankfully, no."

He smiled, and she brushed her hair back behind her ears.

"You need to rest." He said it as if that was the last thing he wanted her to do.

She didn't want to rest. Standing on tiptoes, she put her hands on either side of his grizzly face and brought his mouth to hers. He hesitated for a moment and then returned her kiss.

She pressed herself into him, moaning as his tongue teased hers. As he nibbled her bottom lip, she felt a hot fervour cascade through her. She had never asked for sex before, but this man made her feel confident and sexy, and downright brazen.

Her hands pushed his leather jacket off his shoulders.

Quinn laughed. "You know what you want."

"Yes." Her hands went to his belt buckle, forcing her unsure fingers to work. She undid the clasp and unzipped his jeans.

His cock sprang free. He clutched her hair in his hands.

Watching his face, she noticed a small smile play about his lips.

She reached out, touching his penis, then closing her fingers about him, his skin softer than she'd imagined and cool under her touch.

She watched his face lose some of the usual tension as her hand slid up his shaft; she cupped his smooth, shaven balls.

He put a firm hand on her shoulder, and for a moment, her belly tightened, afraid of his rejection. He pushed harder, and she sank to the floor, the cool hardwood smooth under her knees.

Licking her lips, she brought his shaft to her mouth and tried to take him all in. She sputtered, tears springing to her eyes.

"Relax your jaw, swallow around my cock and breathe through your nose." His voice seemed far away, but his hand in her hair kept her connected to him.

She tried again, this time taking all of him deep into her mouth, so his head bumped the back of her throat.

He tasted salty on her tongue. Simone swallowed and slowly slid her tongue up and down his cock. Hearing him hiss encouraged her. Increasing her speed, she ran her tongue along the underside of his firm cock. She felt his muscles relax, and a delight shot through her at making him lose control.

"Simone." His fist wrapped around her hair, and he tugged.

She went with his motions, going up and down on his cock. A coil of desire formed in her belly as his control became clear. Her pussy gushed as she moved her head up and down on his cock, her hands gripping his strong hips.

"Enough." His hand pulled her head away until she eased her lips off him.

"Sorry. I wanted to give you—" She looked down, not knowing how to finish the sentence; she'd been carried away by the moment.

"If I had let you continue, I would have fucked your mouth, and I would rather fuck your pussy."

God, that deep timbre of his, sent her pulse racing. Anticipation flared along her skin. She ached for him, with the intensity that matched his voce.

She followed his hands as he guided her off the floor.

He nudged her onto the cool leather couch. A jolt of electric desire flared in her as his body covered hers.

He kissed her neck, her back arched as his lips fell on hers, his tongue circling hers. No one had ever made her feel this kind of burning desire before. She circled his neck with her arms, pushing at him, her fingers digging into his shoulders. She wanted him. And she wanted to take everything he would give her.

"Let's get these clothes off you." His voice commanded; her pussy clenched in response.

She reached for the hem on her shirt. Quinn closed his hands over hers.

"Let me."

Leisurely, he lifted the black sparkly top, revealing her black, lacy demi-bra. He palmed her breasts over the fabric. She moaned; and lifted her hips off the couch.

"Are you feeling up to this?" Quinn gently slid his fingers along her cuts.

"Yes!" Simone cried.

"Your impatience will not help you."

His fingers skimmed the waistline of her skirt, and then he slid it down her legs.

The heat in her core rose to searing levels. Simone reached for his hand.

"Where do you want this?"

"Anywhere."

"Here?" His hand tugged her hair.

"Yes."

"You've become needy for my touch." He sounded pleased.

God yes, she was drenched with need and desperation, and she didn't care. She wanted him to ease the burning in her core with those fiery waves of pleasure he'd given her last time.

Simone arched, swaying her hips back and forth, thankful her panties were already off. Thinking about being in the restaurant made her wet.

"Do you want my hand here?" He put his palm over her pussy. Simone thrashed from side to side.

"Yes!" She shouted the word with her whole being.

A slow smile spread across Quinn's face. Her pulse raced at how predatory it made him look.

His hand came over her mound.

"Yes, there!"

She squirmed, trying to incite his hand, his fingers into moving.

"It's a very nice invitation."

He unfastened the clasp on her bra and discarded that with the rest of her clothes.

"Please."

He raised his eyebrows and hovered a finger inches away from her clit. Rising off the couch, she jerked her pussy up to his finger.

He snapped it back. "I want to slap your cunt."

12

CHAPTER TWELVE

G od, her pulse sprinted at the intensity of his glare. In the far corner of her mind, she wondered if this was the appropriate reaction after having a brick thrown at her, but Quinn had busted through her walls of acceptability, and she wanted more.

"Simone?"

Flutters pulsed low in her stomach; her breath caught in her throat. He offered another new idea, and she craved it with hungry anticipation.

"Any objections?"

Wetness slicked the skin between her thighs, her need growing so great she thought she would combust from the throb of it.

"Do it, Quinn."

His dominance inspired her, compelled her to say yes to the things she read about, but it was how he looks at her as if she meant something, as if she was desirable, that melted her insides.

"Yes, Quinn."

His cool hand grabbed her arm. "Sit on the back of the couch. Spread your legs wide.

She followed his instructions.

"Good, wider."

The soft, buttery leather was cold on her ass, making her hiss at the sharp contrast. His heated gaze on her, as he grabbed her thigh, made her pussy gush. He flicked the tip of her clit hard.

Sparks flew through her core, her muscles tightened low in her belly, and a gasp burst free as her legs clamped close.

"Keep them open." Quinn's hand pressed them wide. Her pulse raced, her heart skipping beats. He brought his arm back and his palm slapped her pussy. One, two, three. She rocked forward. A scream escaped her as his palm came away.

"You liked it." His eyes darkened; a small smile curved about his lips.

"Yes! More." The word flew out of her lips.

"Good girl," Quinn said.

Her nipples tightened, and her clit throbbed. She wanted him deep in her; she wanted him to make her a boneless, blissful mess. Simone threw her head back. She needed his cock in her this second.

His next slap connected with her clit, and that jolted her. Her body folded over, her hands came up, blocking his palm. Heat raced through her, and she panted.

"Back in position. Unless you want me to stop?"

"No!" Simone brought her hands under and sat up straight, opening her legs. "Perfect."

One step, he was right between her legs.

She moaned as his finger circled her clit. "Quinn, I need more!"

He withdrew his finger, and Simone bit her lip at the absence.

"Are you sure?" Quinn asked, his blue eyes dark.

"Yes!" Her whole body arched toward him.

"Then take it," he whispered. His fingers on her clit were hard and fast. Her nipples hardened as his fingers moved, hooked deep within her folds and found her G-spot.

Simone threw her head back, her body pulsed.

"You're gushing wet." Quinn held his finger to her mouth, and automatically, she parted her lips. He rubbed his finger on her bottom lip, and she tasted herself.

"I need you," Simone said.

Lightly, his fingers tapped her pussy, and the teasing touch drove her wild. A flush crept up from the swell of her breasts.

"Please," she whimpered. Her pussy throbbed so hard her entire body blazed.

"Ask for it." Quinn stopped his hand, inches from connecting to her heat.

Simone thrust forward, and her head lolled down. "Please, Quinn, slap my pussy again."

"My pleasure." He swung his hand forward, his palm connected with her swollen flesh.

Simone screamed, her pussy tingled, releasing a gush of wetness.

"So hot." Quinn swallowed the rest of her scream, dipped his head, and laid soft kisses between her breasts as she shuddered with the aftershocks. He took one nipple in his mouth and sucked on it long and hard.

A scorching wave of pleasure spiked through her. Quinn nipped her nipple, lapping at it leisurely with his tongue.

"That's it, baby. Open right up for me." Quinn took the other nipple in his mouth and brushed her clit teasingly with his finger, making slow, lazy circles.

"Quinn," Simone panted, her body bowed towards his mouth.

His soft chuckle vibrated around her breast, and he added another finger, pumping in and out, sending a tremor through her centre. She needed more of him, wanted him deep inside her.

He came away from her breast, his eyes roaming every inch of her. "You are a feast for my eyes, for my mouth. God Simone, I'm so hard for you."

This man... she didn't know if she could handle him. But she wanted him to take his fill of her.

His fingers stilled, ever so close to where she wanted them. "I want to make you come again." His breath tickled her ear.

Her hands slid over his back. She titled her neck back, her head hitting the wall as he lapped, licked, and kissed her searing flesh.

"Yes. Yes. Yes." She panted the word out, heat cascading through her body.

"Yes, what?"

His hand stilled, and she cried out at his absence.

"Yes, Quinn."

Quinn plunged a finger deep inside her. A whimper escaped her lips, and her head turned back and forth, her fingers digging into the cushions, trying to find purchase, wanting him deeper.

"Look at me."

With an effort, Simone turned her head and opened her eyes.

"That's it, take what I give you, now." Simone wanted more pressure, wanted more intensity. So she arched up at him, and he stood impassive.

"Greedy girl."

In the next moment, his mouth came down hard on her cunt, making Simone gasp as his fingers spread her pussy lips and his tongue flicked over her swollen clit.

And it was too much. But as the heat of his mouth raked over her body, as his hands held her in place, Simone wanted to meet his challenge. He told her to take it; she wanted to obey.

This strong, experienced man knew exactly how to light her up in all the right places. He licked, lapped, and nipped until Simone thought she would implode with need.

"Your pussy is paradise." His words struck a match for her already burning fire.

"You do this to me," she said. "You make me hot and needy." Someone made a mewling sound she didn't think could have come from her. But it must have.

He grabbed the hem of his shirt, pulled it up over his head, revealing his firm abs and the hard planes of his body.

His cock was hard, pressing against his belly.

"Oh." Simone came forward, reached out for it.

Quinn gently pushed her back. "I'm glad you like what you see, but you stay there."

He grinned at her and rolled on a condom.

"Not fair."

"You look so cute when you pout."

His powerful hands lifted her from the back of the couch to the cool cushions. He kneeled above her, nudging her legs wider apart, his weight making the cushions sink.

His lips met hers for a kiss, his body pressing into hers. Simone moaned as his hardness pressed against her core.

"Please, Quinn."

"I love to hear you beg."

Simone didn't know why she found his control and demands such a turn-on, but she did, and right now, she didn't care, she wanted to please him.

"Yes, please."

Above her, Quinn smiled, his eyes lit with desire, making her feel more heated.

"Good girl." He held his cock in one hand, poised at her entrance.

He entered her with the tip of his hard shaft. Simone's body bucked and thrashed in protest. Her legs came around his waist, urging him deeper.

"You are so stunning right now." His hands lightly held her shoulders.

He slowly sank another inch into her and Simone felt a scream rise in her throat. With his finger, he circled her clit.

"God! Yes..." Simone breathed out.

"And I need you." In one smooth stroke, he dove his hard length all the way in. Simone yelped as she felt her walls stretched around his girth.

Quinn sped up his rhythm, and she rocked hard under him, her legs around his muscular back, taking his strokes, taking every inch of him.

Her head swam, dizzy with the mounting pleasure. She needed him to take her over the edge, and she wasn't sure she could withstand much more anticipation.

"Hold on to me, baby."

He held her, stroking her hard and fast. Held her, and she closed her eyes, getting lost in the smooth rhythm. He felt so good.

"Come for me, now." His command tipped her over. Simone's body tightened, then the power of her orgasm towed her under.

"Quinn." She drove her nails into his back. Another long stroke from him, and she felt his release as his powerful body wrapped around hers. She shivered, his sweat coated body making her cool.

Quinn shifted his weight, pulling her on his lap; he held her, caressing the back of her neck. "Baby, I want to do all the dirty, naughty things to you."

A look of regret cast a shadow on his beautiful features, and a pang of sorrow washed over Simone. This couldn't last. He was the only man she'd ever felt safe with, the only man she'd ever felt could care for her, and he would not stick around. But she couldn't take back how she felt, and she promised herself she would never fall in love again.

Quinn brushed the hair off her face, tracing a finger along her jaw. "You don't know what I want to do to you."

"Tell me."

"I want to tie you to a St. Andrew's cross and flog you," Quinn said. "I want to paddle your ass red and have you scream my name. I want to fill your ass and make you beg for more. I want to do things to you that make you a boneless mess."

"God, Quinn," Simone moaned.

Quinn laughed gently, eased himself out of her, and unsheathed his cock.

"I want to do it again and again. I can't get enough of you, Simone."

She gripped him tight as his words sent off a fresh wave of desire in her. He moved across the room, washed his hands, opened the fridge.

"Can we do more now?" A blaze of adrenaline raced through her veins. She didn't want this to be the end, to night. She wanted all the things he talked about.

"I wanted to hear you say that." Quinn passed her a bottle of water. His mouth collided with hers and Simone threw her arms around his back, pressing herself into him.

"Let's move to the bed."

God, the smile he gave her was like the baby sun melting ice in winter, a flash of unexpected brightness. Her skin buzzed as Quinn's palm pressed against her back. From the nightstand, he took out a fresh condom, rolled it on.

"On your hands and knees, on the bed."

Her stomach flip-flopping, Simone scrambled to do what he asked.

Her palms pressed down on the soft sheets. She glanced at him over her shoulder, flutters in her stomach raced as he dug in his leather bag, taking out a bottle of lube. He brought out a black silicone butt plug and Simone gasped.

"Quinn—"

"We'll take this nice and slow. I want you to experience this, Simone. Breathe." He set down the plug, near her calve, she shivered slightly as she felt the silicone against her skin. He rubbed circles on her ass. "Can you trust me?"

"Yes, Quinn," she exhaled.

He squirted lube between his hands.

"Breathe." He rubbed circles on her ass, his finger pressing against her back entrance. His warm lube coated fingers, made her relax. "That's it. Arch against my touch, Simone."

She clutched the sheets as she felt his finger slide against her anus, she gripped the sheets. "Quinn, I don't know..."

"Do you want to stop?"

He moved a palm over her ass, caressing her. His touch, so sure and warm, reassured her. "No. I want to continue.""Good girl. Let me in, Simone."

She breathed and as his finger slid past her tight ring of muscles, tingles rippled through her.

She gasped, moved forward, away from his touch.

"Get back in position. This is going to feel so good when you relax." His tone commanded her back to her hands and knees.

Quinn's finger stroked her, moving back, and her skin flared with warmth, making her want more. Heat rose to the surface, prickling her across the surface of her skin, and the next moment she rocked back and forth. He pulled his finger out, and she bit the side of her cheek.

"Now you're warmed-up," Quinn said. "Grab your ass cheeks and spread for me, Simone."

Oh, God. This seemed too much, too far. She swallowed. The thought of opening for him, a ripple of anticipation raced through her, mixed with her nerves. Quinn pressed his hand against her ass.

"Open for me, Simone."

She hesitated, wondering if this was too far. She swallowed.

"Use a safeword or spread for me, Simone, now."

Quinn's palm on her ass reassured her, and a moment later, she spread her ass cheeks.

"Feel this." Something cool and long rolled between her ass cheeks. "This medium-sized plug, and it's going in."

Simone whimpered, arching back toward Quinn's.

"Push back, and this will slide right in Quinn rubbed his palm over her ass and her tensed muscles started to relax under his determined touch.

Quinn reached between her legs, his fingers sweeping over her clitoris.

"You're thinking too much. Breathe in and out, Simone."

Slowly, she did and she felt the plug slide past her ring of muscles and her legs wanted to close on the unfamiliar sensation.

God, she felt spread wide open. Vulnerable. Wet and ready, Simone moved back and forth as hot sensations pricked her skin. She felt wholly submissive.

"So damn hot." His fingers plunged in her folds and Simone arched towards his touch, wanting more, wanting his touch deeper.

"Quinn." His fingers ignored her aching clit, and she tried to wiggle for his touch.

"In time." He slapped her ass, and Simone moaned, her hard nipples scraping the bed sheets.

Quinn's smooth torso aligned with her back and she gasped as his hips pressed down on her ass cheeks, his hard cock slid, inch by inch into her ready pussy. With every thrust of his, her breath released in a shuddering exhale. She moved her hips back towards him, needing his hard length to fill her in just the right spot. It loomed out of reach.

The weight of his strong body pressed against the unfamiliar feel of the plug, making her feel so full. She pushed back against him, whimpering.

"Beautiful," Quinn said. He moved deep within her, slowly. Her hands clutched the sheets with each stroke. God, she felt so needy. And so wet.

"Please." The throaty tone of her voice surprised her.

"Yes, my sweet sub," Quinn said. His hand grabbed her hair, and she moaned as he increased his tempo, drilling into her with each thrust.

Simone gritted her teeth, wondering if he was testing her or enjoying himself with this agonizing torture, and decided it was both.

"Yes!" His fingers finally found her clit and quenched her need, as his cock drilled into her.

He pulled on her hair and pinched her clit, and her vision grew hazy.

"Now, Simone," his cool voice increased the heat. A path of fire lit in her core, down to her toes, up, somewhere beyond her.

One long and deep thrust, one more tug on her hair and she screamed. Her head swam.

"Yes, good girl." She shivered as his lips trailed down the back of her neck, her body convulsing from the aftershocks. He held her hips until her body stilled and she opened her eyes, smiling at him. He returned her smile.

She hummed with satisfaction, luxuriating in the buzz of it. Quinn eased out her.

"I'm going to take the plug out of you now."

"No, I can do it."

His hand came around hers. "I'm taking care of you."

The intensity in his eyes had her exhaling in acceptance. "Okay."

"That's a good girl."

He eased out of her, pulled a sheet up over her, and disappeared into the bathroom.

God, she wanted to stay in this orgasmic bliss for always, with this man at her side.

"Spread." He pressed the warm washcloth between her legs, brought it over her ass. He kissed the base of her spine. "You did so well."

God, his careful clean-up of her twisted her insides as he gently cleaned her thighs and pussy.

"Thank you."

"Simone..." his blue eyes pierced hers, and her heart lunged.

"Quinn," she said.

He slid in next to her, pulling her head on his chest.

As she snuggled under the covers, warmth infused her every limb, and she couldn't imagine feeling happier.

If he stayed, she thought before sleep took her, I would be happier if he stayed.

13
CHAPTER THIRTEEN

With a curse, Quinn tore himself away from the bedroom.

He wished he could stay next to Simone, with her soft body spooned next to his, inhaling her scent and feeling her silky hair tickle his chest. But his self-appointed mission needed his attention. Time was running out.

He kissed her forehead, brushed his hand through her hair, and threw on a pair of shorts.

In the kitchen, he flipped open his laptop and ran another search on Liam Boucher. He needed to find out more about Simone's ex. The clock was counting down.

His mouth went dry over a lump in his throat. Damn, he missed Jordan. If he were here, his best friend would hear all the facts and then spit out the one thing that would make the missing connection apparent to Quinn's strategic brain.

The search results on Liam's name brought up a lot of press about his real estate mogul mother. A few clicks brought up pictures of him and Simone at charity events sponsored by Marion's company.

Quinn changed the parameters of the search to eliminate Marion's name and kept reading.

On page five of the search results, he found out about Liam's business.

From the article Quinn read, it was a franchise that, according to the article, "brought science into the classroom." He found the name and address of Liam's business partner and plugged it into his phone for later.

Quinn stared out the windows at the mountain range towering above the city, the sky lighting as dawn broke for a long moment. His jaw clenched, thinking about the person he had to call.

Fury vibrated through his being. Forcing himself to move, he grabbed the jump rope hanging in the closet, along with some free weights. He furiously pounded the floor, losing himself in a gruelling rhythm. After half an hour, he had a decent sweat going.

He wiped himself off with a towel and punched in Logan's digits.

"Do you ever sleep?"

His best friend's voice was husky, and Quinn wondered if he had a girl in his bed.

"Morning. Give me Erik's number."

Quinn heard rustling and the closing of a door.

"What do you need? Can I act as a messenger?"

"I need to talk to the fucker myself. Someone threw a brick aimed at Simone's head last night. Xander sent him out to the scene. I need to hear him tell me about it directly."

"He's the best at reconnaissance."

The bastard was, except for that one time that cost Jordan his life.

"Logan!"

"Okay. This chick must mean something."

"I'm trying to keep her safe. I need to find out who is after her. Send me his number."

"Sending his deets over. Anything else?"

"Can you run down JayJay Harris?"

"Consider it done."

Quinn clicked off and, before he changed his mind, jabbed the numbers on his phone.

"Yeah?"

Instantly, hearing Erik's voice caused the rage to bubble over. Quinn threw his phone across the floor, thankful for his military-grade case.

He needed another round of jump rope.

Ten minutes later, he turned on the faucet on the kitchen sink, he ducked his head right under the cold water.

His breathing slowed; his fists unclenched. He found his phone across the room, under the table and hit redial.

After hearing the click, Quinn exhaled.

"Tell me everything you saw at Simone's last night."

"Uncommon grey-black colour on the brick. They wrapped the note around the brick with four orange elastics. The words were hand-printed in sharpie."

"What else?" He pushed the words through his gritted teeth.

"Most likely someone threw it by climbing on the neighbour's half garden wall. I walked around Simone's yard and found footprints in the back bushes, made by a large boot with a high heel. I found a ring at the end of the drive."

"Send me a picture of the ring," Quinn barked.

His phone beeped just as he ended the call.

"Xander, what is it?"

The clock on the stove read twenty after five.

"Mulberry is in town and has requested our services for personal security. They asked for you and Nick specifically."

A vice gripped him; he appreciated Axis Management's belief in him, but he couldn't.

"We could use you. Try this one job."

The muffled sound of the shower coming on reached him. He threw a couch cushion across the room, watched as it bounced off the window to the million-dollar view. Only a dumbass would want to leave this.

"Nope."

Xander hung up before he could throw the phone.

Quinn smirked. He knew his friend was pissed at him for not committing to another year under contract.

With all his energy expelled, he flopped on the couch and mentally ran through everything he knew so far, which was little. The scent of peach and vanilla caused him to open his eyes. Simone stood next to him.

"Good morning."

Damn, her presence halted his downward thought spiral. He threaded his fingers through her hand.

"You look all fresh and delicious." He pulled her down for a kiss she giggled. She had on a grey T-shirt with the word LOVE across the front and a pair of yoga pants. The woman could wear a paper bag and still look sexy.

"It's lucky that I left my bag here yesterday. You distracted me, but the brick freaks me out a lot."

He didn't want her to be upset but was glad to see her rattled. She had to take these threats seriously. "Most women I know would be freaked out by strange text messages and a brick thrown at them. Why do you disregard your safety so much?" Quinn pulled her beside him.

Simone bit her lip, smoothed out her pants, and shrugged at him. "It's stupid."

"Nothing you tell me is stupid. Spit it out, Simone." Quinn placed his palm on her thigh.

"My father got death threats when I was going into my third year of high school, and my entire world stopped, Quinn. I wasn't allowed to go out of the house. My dad didn't let me go to school. This kept going for two years, and it turned out the supposed threat against him was another surgeon at the hospital."

Quinn chewed the inside of his lip. Hearing her story, he could think of a few things wrong in how they'd handled that threat, and if she had to live through that as a teenager, no wonder she didn't take the threatening text messages seriously.

"I'm happy that threat turned out to be wrong, Simone, and it sounds like they went overboard in their security measures. But you're on TV, anyone in the world can watch you through streaming. You need to take your security seriously. Has the studio offered media training of any sort? Have you taken a self-defence class?"

Simone shook her head. "No. When I went to college, it was like the cows being let out for the winter. I studied hard, but I went clubbing every moment I could."

Quinn kissed her glossy lips. "You are not a cow, not even a happy one."

Simone laughed. "I felt exactly like those cows do after being stuck at home for two years. The studio sent out a sheet of things we shouldn't post on social media, and no, I have taken no self-defence classes."

Quinn grunted. "One of our bodyguards, Janette, teaches women's self-defence. I'll send you the info. I'm going to grab a quick shower. The garage is dropping your car off in about an hour."

"I'll get caught up with Ava while you're in the shower. I feel bad that I haven't checked in on her."

"We've been busy." Quinn kissed her.

He quickly washed, shaved, dressed, and slid a condom into his wallet. At the rate they were going, he wanted to have it on his person. When he got out of the shower, Simone had her bag by the door.

"The car should be here in ten minutes. They just texted me."

She gave him a small smile. He didn't want her to leave, either. "What if I come to your place with you? I can follow you along."

"No, that's okay. I need to walk through my door at some point."

"Dinner then?"

She raised her eyebrows. "Yes, I would like that."

"Good," Quinn said.

His heart hitched. He knew he wasn't ready to let her go, but he couldn't stay. He had today to find out who hired him to destroy her.

A chime rang out and Quinn opened the door.

"Good morning! Hi Simone! I'll see you later this afternoon for the interview!" Kayleigh barrelled past them, her hands full with a tray of iced coffees and a pastry box.

"Kayleigh, what are you doing here?" Quinn glared at his sister.

"We need to talk, big brother. No more putting it off."

"That's my cue to leave." Simone slipped her feet into her kitten heels.

"Yes! I'll text you the address later! Wait, have a muffin." Kayleigh tried to put the box down but almost toppled the tray of drinks. Quinn reached out and took the tray from her.

"My hero," Kayleigh said. She raised her eyebrows at Simone, giving her a wink.

Simone's peal of laughter made Quinn smile, despite himself.

"Those look good," Simone said, peering into the box.

"They're from the muffin shop on the corner. Cinnamon coconut carrot muffin?"

"Why not?"

"And have an iced coffee." Kayleigh put the cup in Simone's hand.

"Thanks. See you later." Simone smiled.

"I'm going to walk Simone out," Quinn picked up her bag.

"Make sure you come back!" Kayleigh waved at them.

"What are you laughing at?" Quinn asked.

"She's so much fun."

"Try having her as a sister." He put her hand in his.

Quinn pressed the button for the elevator and then pushed her against the wall. The cup of ice coffee cool against his waist, the paper bag crinkled against his back as she brought her arms around him.

She squealed. His hands framed either side of her face. He roughly tugged her to him and devoured her berry pink glossy lips.

Her body squirmed against his, and Quinn had the urge to through her over his shoulder caveman style, back to the suite and kick his sister out. His tongue found hers, and he plunged into her mouth, hard and fast. He couldn't get enough of her, and that was a problem.

As the elevator dinged, he released her mouth, brushing her hair behind her ears.

"I needed to kiss you."

The doors whizzed open. Quinn strode towards her until he had her pressed against the far wall of the elevator.

"My bag!" Simone laughed.

Quinn cursed, grabbed her bag before the doors closed. One look at her flushed face and dilated eyes made his cock hard enough to stab concrete. He reached out and pushed the stop button.

"Quinn!" Part laughter, part cry, and it urged him on.

He nuzzled her neck, kissed her creamy skin. He took the iced coffee from her hands, set it in the corner with her bag.

"I need you. Now." His hands tugged her yoga pants down.

"Quinn, we can't," Simone protested but stepped out of her pants.

"We can, baby." He sank two fingers into her folds, finger fucking her hard until his fingers grew soaked with her juices.

"Help me out of my jeans."

Simone bucked against him at his command, her sure hands on his waistband, unzipping his fly. Cupping her with one hand, he pushed his jeans down over his ass.

"Grab my shoulders. Don't let go."

His mouth crashed into hers. As he lifted her, he felt her legs circle him, and his hands went under her ass. No woman ever had brought out his dominance like she did. Damn, he liked it. More than he should.

"I can't do this," Simone breathed heavily against his neck.

"Yes, you can. I've got you." Quinn kissed her throat, his hands squeezing her ass checks. "Do you want to stop?"

Her eyes flew open, her hips arched. "No!"

"Then we are doing this. I want you to scream so loud that the walls shake."

"More, Quinn, please!" she panted.

"There you are, being greedy again."

This close to her, he noticed the gold flecks in her brown eyes, the curve of her pert nose, and the sweat forming on the top of her lips as he grounded his hips into her, his hands holding her up against the wall.

"Keep your eyes open. I want to see you come," he said.

While he supported her with his knee and hand, he put his other hand on his hard cock, the crest already dripping.

He positioned his cockshead at her entrance, dragging it around her wetness. "Look at you, swollen and ready."

"Need you," Simone said breathlessly.

He threw his head back and gritted his teeth, part of his brain wishing that she wasn't this desirable, that she didn't ignite him to this passionate frenzy of wanting to consume her.

"Needed you so bad, I had to fuck you here."

A trail of fire licked up his back. His balls tightened, and with one hand holding her thigh, the other wrapped around her, he hammered into her. Her pussy felt molten as it gripped his cock.

Her nails on his shoulders drove him harder; feeling her breasts bounce against his chest made him growl.

She pulled him closer, clawing at his shoulders. He watched, fixated, as her eyes rolled, her entire body tensed.

He plowed into her so hard and fast that she let out a breathless gasp.

"I want to stay here forever in your sweet pussy," he growled.

One last long hard stroke, and she yelped, screamed his name as her orgasm rolled over her. He came, his body shuddering at the release. She kissed him hungrily, and he reciprocated, brushing damp hair off her face.

"Simone."

Her dewy gaze seared him, and Quinn didn't know how he could leave her. If only things were different. He held her until her pulse slowed and kissed her on the forehead.

He set her down gently on her feet, grabbed the napkins around the iced coffee, and gently used them to blot between her legs. Taking off the condom, he wrapped it in the bundle of napkins.

"That was a first I didn't expect to happen." A blush painted her cheeks as she laid her hand on his bicep.

"Glad you enjoyed the ride."

She threw her head back and laughed, and his heart twisted in his chest.

Damn this pure, kind woman. She couldn't be for him. He would ruin her with his baggage. He tucked himself back in and helped her straighten out her clothing.

He kissed her hard on her mouth. "Ready?"

"I guess we have to get out of here."

"There's tonight." Quinn traced her lips with his finger.

He hit the emergency button; the elevator lurched.

Simone reached for his hand, and his fingers curled around hers.

The doors opened, and he led her through the private hallway and out through the lobby. He held open the sleek glass door, the sun assaulting his eyes. He didn't want to say goodbye, not now, and not for an hour. He wanted one more dinner with her. Maybe questioning Gerald Sommers, her ex-husband's former business partner, would help him figure out who wanted this woman who had found her way under the shields to his heart, dead.

"There's my car."

He opened the car door for her.

"See you later."

"Can't wait."

She put on her seat belt; his lips brushed hers. He closed the door and returned her wave.

14

CHAPTER FOURTEEN

Stuck in traffic, Quinn glanced at his phone, considered calling his sister, not liking how he'd left things with her. The moment he'd got back to the suite, Kayleigh had grabbed his arm, insisted he sit down while she told him about her new idea.

Quinn crossed his arms over his chest and waited her out.

"I read this book about a woman who converted an old van into a bookstore, and now she drives around from town to town. Don't you think that's awesome?"

"You want to open a bookstore?" Quinn asked.

"I am not going to open a bookstore! A teahouse that serves fancy sandwiches and little, tiny desserts. It's open at night and doesn't serve alcohol. Isn't that the best idea you've ever heard? You don't drink. Don't you want somewhere to take your girlfriend that doesn't have alcohol on the menu?"

"No. I order iced tea," Quinn said.

"But wouldn't you want something exciting? Like lavender rose tea? Or bubble tea?"

Quinn shook his head at her. "Kayleigh, no. You know I wouldn't. Bubble tea isn't my scene."

"Okay, you wouldn't, but maybe Simone would. Think about it," she pleaded, her green eyes alight with excitement. "People who don't drink need fancy sandwiches too!"

And to make this dream of hers happen, she needed ten thousand dollars.

It wasn't the money... or *just* the money he often paid her rent and kept her fridge stocked. It was another ill-thought-out plan.

"What about the publication you are working for?"

"I can do both," she said. Her voice broke, and she got that pouty look on her face Quinn knew all too well.

But she couldn't do both. She did many things, just not at once, and often ended up quitting everything because all those plates she juggled eventually came crashing down and overwhelmed her.

"Kayleigh, I think you have enough with the publication right now. You can think about it again in a few months," Quinn said, keeping his tone gentle.

"You don't tell me what to do. I'm not one of your whores." Tears splashed down her face as she gathered her things.

"Kayleigh—"

She flung off his touch. "You never support my ideas!"

"Kayleigh, be rational for one moment here," Quinn said.

"You don't love me!" she yelled at him and stormed out.

Quinn sighed. He never knew how to handle Kayleigh, but he wished he had done a better job of it.

Now he rolled down the window, trying to keep himself awake. Traffic started moving, and a few moments later, he pulled into a new townhouse behind a motorcycle parked in the driveway. He rapped on the door once, twice, three times. He felt like the big bad wolf, ready to blow.

"Yeah?" The door opened to reveal Gerald Sommers, with a beer in one hand and a cigarette in the other. He was lanky, with grey hair and a pierced lip, not what came to mind when one thought of "scientist."

"Gerald Sommers? I'm wondering if I can talk to you about Liam Boucher."

"That backstabbing asshole. I hope he's rotting in hell!" Gerald went to slam the door and Quinn stuck his foot in the way. Gerald Sommers pushed on the door, but Quinn braced his arm against the door.

"Things ended badly between you two," Quinn said.

"He disappeared one day, poof gone, and I was on the line for one hundred and fifty thousand dollars. That bitch of his didn't help either," Gerald spat out.

"You leave Simone alone!" Quinn's hand clutched his shirt before he thought better about it.

The man wheezed heavily and tapped Quinn's wrist. Reluctantly, Quinn let him go.

"Who the fuck are you?" Gerald yelled.

"Someone who is looking out for Simone."

His gaze softened. "She's in trouble?"

"Yes," Quinn gritted out.

At the mention of Simone being in trouble, Gerald took two steps back, ran his hand through his hair. Quinn started to re-evaluate his assessment of him.

"God, who would want to hurt her?"

"That's what I'm trying to figure out. You lost a lot of money. That's enough to make many people pretty upset, maybe even enough to go after someone."

Gerald held up on hand. "Whoa, I'd never hurt Simone!"

Brushing the outstretched arm aside, Quinn got right up in the other man's face. "Then why did you call her a bitch?"

Gerald shook his head. "You got it all wrong, and you might as well come in to hear my side of the story."

Quinn nodded and followed Gerald inside, surprised at the gleaming hardwood floors and meticulously clean living room with two huge easy chairs on either side of a fireplace.

"You want a beer?"

"Sure," Quinn said. He didn't drink the stuff, but he knew accepting it would make Gerald more at ease. Hospitality was something he'd learned from Fiona. Jordan's mom was the one everyone went to for comfort, and she was the one who taught him how to get people to open up. Accepting and offering food and drink went a long way in building a bridge.

The far wall of the living room displayed degrees from three different universities, and under that, a host of awards.

"Nice trophies," Quinn said.

Gerald put an ice-cold beer in his hand. "Got no better place to put them now that I'm out of work. Are you sure someone is out to hurt Simone?"

"Yeah. Do you know where Liam is?"

"Nope. He stopped returning my calls months ago. He knew he was on the hook for the money."

"Why wouldn't he give it to you? From what I know, he was well off."

"Oh, Liam has more money than God," Gerald said. "But his mother controls every dime. She's the reason he left everything, tired of her control."

"Are you sure?" Quinn asked. It surprised him to hear this because Liam Boucher wasn't an uneducated man.

Gerald ran his hand through his hair and plopped himself in the armchair. "Marion didn't want Liam to go through with the franchise because she thought that teaching chemistry in a fun way was too pedestrian for him. Liam wanted out of the labs and didn't want to teach in academia."

"Were he and Simone happy?"

Gerald frowned. "They weren't obviously unhappy, but there were no sparks. I thought that Liam might have played for the other team, but one night after I had too many, he gently told me no." He looked away.

"That must have hurt. Maybe you were jealous of Simone?"

"No. I felt a little sorry for her. She gave her heart all over the place. One year I had the flu but had to meet a publication deadline. She not only sent me over food but cleaners too. She knew how an untidy space drove me crazy. She always lent a hand."

"Did Marion like her?" Quinn asked.

"Liam wouldn't have married her if she didn't. I'm sorry about my reaction at the door. You turning up was a shock."

Quinn wondered if Gerald was putting him on for a moment, but the sincerity in his voice when he spoke about Simone convinced him that the guy was being truthful.

"Marion liked Simone because Simone had no backbone. She would drop everything for her and come and do whatever Marion needed. The money sucks, and I'll get over it, but I miss Liam as a friend, and I hope he *is* living a better life."

Pacing, Quinn took another look at the trophy wall.

"Did Liam just up and leave?"

"It was sudden." Gerald nodded. "It was right before his mother's big charity dinner, too. He never showed up; Marion was livid. Simone must have been heartbroken, but she put on a smile and got Marion through the evening."

Quinn's heart twisted. He really had no business with a woman like her. She was too together, too classy for the likes of him. "Poor Simone," he muttered.

"He left a note."

"What did the note say?"

"Something like, sorry, off to find myself."

Quinn blinked. "Wow."

"Yeah. But if your mother was as controlling as Marion, maybe you would write something so blasé after getting the courage to change your life at twenty-five."

Fair point. Quinn wondered if Marion blamed Simone for Liam leaving, but Marion had stood by her side this year, according to Simone.

Quinn paced for a moment.

"Do you know JayJay Harris?"

"Oh yeah. He kept calling me and harassing me, asking if Liam had given me back the money. I guess Marion wanted it back or wanted to know where Liam had gone with it or something. JayJay wouldn't stop calling."

"Who is he?" According to what his fellow Bandit Brothers had found out, JayJay Harris was an admin assistant at a lawyer's office.

"Marion's assistant. He does everything for her,"

A cold stone lodged in Quinn's stomach. "Her assistant?"

"Yeah. He's a character, Carson is his actual name. JayJay is his stage name for his stand-up comedy act. He does this whole bit about working for a lawyer."

Fuck. Quinn bit the inside of his cheek but felt himself break out into a sweat.

This should have been an easy puzzle to sort out, and instead, he had let all the clues that pointed to Marion slip through his fingers.

"Thanks for your time." Quinn put the untouched beer on a shelf and held out his hand to the scientist. Gerald shook Quinn's hand. "Yeah. Don't worry about it. Make sure Simone is okay."

"You can count on it," Quinn said.

Back in his truck, Quinn sat hunched over his steering wheel. This was a clusterfuck. He took a deep breath and tried to slow down his thoughts.

Marion wanted to send her former daughter-in-law up in flames. Why?

And why couldn't he have seen that before now? Because his head wasn't in the game.

When Simone finds out about Marion's betrayal, it's going to devastate her. And Quinn would do everything he could to spare her that pain. The realization spread through his body, making him exhale. With Simone, he felt like something other than a screw-up.

He was glad his sister was keeping Simone occupied with the interview for the rest of the afternoon, and he would keep her beside him at night. And tomorrow, he would show up, act as if he was going to set the house on fire, in case Marion had a backup plan.

Quinn's heart clenched in his chest; his palms were sweating on the steering wheel. He was going to keep Simone safe, no matter what it took.

15

CHAPTER FIFTEEN

Meeting with the police officer to give a statement went smoother than Simone thought it would, even though it felt unsatisfactory. It echoed what Quinn had told her last night. They felt it was a random act of vandalism. For a moment, she considered telling them about the text messages, but she knew Axis Management was on it.

She wanted to call Quinn but brushed it aside. They were consenting adults having fun together. He wasn't her boyfriend.

Simone turned into the parking lot of the fancy grocery store. Remembering how Quinn had held her in place against the elevator wall as he hammered her made her smile. And blush.

She grew warm just thinking about it. If she was honest with herself, she wanted more. More of Quinn, even though he told her he was going. He had to come back. Kayleigh and his friends were here. She planned to invite Quinn over to her place and cook dinner for him. As much as she didn't want to go into her house, it would be easier with him by her side.

She wanted to show him her garden, and a flush crept up her neck, imagining the moonlight hitting his muscular body as he pinned her down on her lounger.

Simone shook herself from her thoughts, realized she had missed a call from Ava. With a recipe and shopping list loaded on her phone, she grabbed a shopping cart and went through the aisles.

In the first year of her marriage, she had tried to cook for Liam one night and ended up setting off all the smoke alarms. Picking up a bitter melon in her hand and eyeing it dubiously, Simone second-guessed her plan. She wanted to do something for Quinn to show him how she felt, and she was kind of curious if her lack of cooking ability came from the fact that she had never tried to cook for anyone she had cared about before. She put the melon in her cart and added two eggplants.

Her excitement grew, and she felt giddy as she chose more things to add to her cart, trying to hurry to make sure she had enough time to go home, put the groceries away, change, and meet Kayleigh for the interview. She had just finished loading the car when Ava's number flashed on her screen for the second time.

"Hi!" Simone exclaimed.

"You sound happy," Ava mumbled.

"Yes! I am. You sound upset. What's wrong?"

"I forgot my make-up bag at the hotel, and I have an early call tomorrow. Can you swing by and get it for me?"

Simone drummed her fingers on her steering wheel. If she had to stop by the hotel and then to Ava's, she would cut the time to meet Kayleigh close and eat into her dinner prep time.

"Please, Simone," Ava begged.

With a sigh, Simone headed in the hotel's direction.

"Okay. I'm on my way. I can't stay long, though."

"You're the best, Simone," Ava said.

She felt guilty because she'd been busy with Quinn having all those naughty things done to her. She hadn't even called Ava the morning after to see if she was all right.

At the hotel, she had to wait behind a huge noisy group of tourists checking in and then longer for the manager to track down where they had put the make-up bag. As quickly as she could, she made her way through the throng of guests, heaved the make-up kit into her car—she'd never known it weighed so much—and then drove across the city to Ava's condo.

Knocking on Ava's door, Simone checked her watch.

If she didn't leave soon, she was going to be late for her interview with Kayleigh.

Ten minutes later, her phone buzzed, hopefully, Ava with an explanation. Simone smiled to see a bunch of happy face emojis from Kayleigh.

Kayleigh was a beam of sunshine next to Quinn's stormy exterior.

The elevators pinged, and Ava appeared in the open door with a towel thrown around her neck. She gave a casual smile as she approached. "Hey Simone, thanks!"

Unlocking her door, Ava gestured to Simone to go in ahead of her.

"Where were you?"

"My running buddy asked me to go around the block," Ava said.

"I've been waiting almost fifteen minutes for you."

"Sorry. I had to run off some stress. You didn't comment on my rug."

"You took my advice. The rug looks great," Simone said.

The deep blue rug fit in perfectly with Ava's retro pieces and dark sage curtains.

"Here, try this. It's a cocktail I made for after a workout."

Ava handed her a glass of something thick and green, the most unappealing drink Simone had ever seen.

"Ew, what's that?"

"It has cucumber juice in it and a little gin. Try it," Ava smiled.

"I don't know, Ava. It looks worse than any of the cocktails we made," Simone said.

"It doesn't have as much booze in it, that's why. Ready for work tomorrow?"

"Yes. Are you?"

"Did you see the new video that I posted?" Ava asked.

"No, I haven't checked my feeds."

Ava's face fell, and Simone felt guilty. She should have checked on Ava sooner. Suppressing her revulsion, Simone sat down at her kitchen table and took a sip of the workout elixir, scrunching her nose.

"It's not gross," Ava said.

Her comment reminded Simone of Quinn telling her she looked cute when she ate gross food, and she blushed.

"Guess what! I took you up on your double dare and had sex with Quinn!"

"What? The guy from the wedding?" Ava pitched forward, gripping the back of the chair so hard her knuckles were white.

"You and Meredith are always telling me to be more adventurous." At the look of shock on her friend's face. Simone wanted to crawl inside herself. She shook her head. No, she wouldn't do that after everything that had happened between her and Quinn. Finally, she felt like she was being true to herself. Maybe Ava was jealous.

"Simone, you hardly know him!"

Simone stared at Ava. This wasn't like her friend. Her stomach lurched, and she felt like she was going to be sick. "Yeah, the guy from the wedding, who *you* encouraged me to bang, remember?"

She stood up, knocking over the green sludge.

"Sorry, I'll clean it up," Simone said. An icy chill swept over her body and Simone grabbed the edge of the table.

"That's so dangerous," Ava said, following her into the kitchen.

"You've slept with people you don't know."

She had told Ava because she wanted her friend to be happy for her, and she couldn't understand why Ava was being judgmental.

"It's just not your usual thing." Ava crossed her arms over her chest. "And besides I think he crashed the reception. I don't remember seeing him at the wedding, and I definitely would have remembered meeting him."

"Maybe it will be now," Simone said. "I got to go. I'm not feeling well." Her face was red, and her stomach kept gurgling. She hadn't eaten much and the drink was too acidic on an empty stomach.

"It doesn't seem like you. You're going to get hurt," Ava said, her arms crossed over her chest.

"I'll take my chances. See you tomorrow."

Quickly, she got in her car. Hot tears gathered in her eyes, and she forced herself to take a few deep breaths. She swiped at her face. It was silly to cry over Ava's reaction.

Two nights ago, she had wished she could be as carefree as Ava and Meredith.

Meeting Quinn and experiencing the hot, kinky sex she had, she felt free to explore those fantasies Liam found perverted, free to be herself.

Heat flashed all over her body and she grew woozy. Yawning, she pulled down the windows and resisted the urge to call Quinn. She wanted to hear his voice, but she would see him after the interview with Kayleigh.

Simone yanked a hard left on the steering wheel, then everything went dark.

16
CHAPTER SIXTEEN

Quinn studied the modest house on the corner of a residential street. "When I asked for back-up, I didn't expect you guys to run surveillance and break into JayJay's house."

Logan slapped him on the back and grinned. "You asked me to run down JayJay. I did. Come inside and see what we've found."

As he followed Logan up three concrete steps, Quinn thought of everything he'd learned from Gerald Sommers, his mind racing, trying to connect the pieces.

In the front hallway, stacks of boxes stood high, nearly touching the ceiling. Quinn found Nick hunched over an open laptop with a bunch of papers spread out on an old coffee table.

The space was open-concept and clean, but other than the appliances, it was bare. "Does Marion not pay her assistant or is he taking off?"

Nick's fingers stopped clacking. He raised an eyebrow over his wire-frame glasses. "How do you know JayJay Harris and Carson Watson are the same person?" Nick asked. "We were going to tell you."

"I had a little chat with a former business partner of Simone's asshole ex. He let me know Carson did stand-up comedy as JayJay Harris. One hell of a way to moonlight."

Logan's fist pumped into the air and held his hand up for a five high. "I knew it! You can't help but do this. You're going to stay."

"This isn't a job," Quinn growled.

"Fine. It's a white knight expedition to save your sweet new sub."

"She's not mine." Quinn glared at his friends.

Nick chuckled, tapping furiously on his keyboards. "I'm working on tracing who sent you that transfer."

"Why does Marion want to set Simone on fire?" Logan asked.

"Gerald said Marion was mad. Liam was working with him. Marion has made a few poor deals lately. The insurance on that house must be huge," Quinn said.

"Yeah, but it's one thing to burn down a house, another to make sure your former daughter-in-law is inside the house while it burns. One can be insurance fraud, the other is murder, and it's a huge jump between the two. It doesn't add up." Logan echoed Quinn's thoughts.

"None of this adds up," Quinn mumbled. "These guys aren't professionals. The deadline is tomorrow, and I haven't received one text or email from them."

"The one thing we know for sure is that they are amateurs. Why don't you just run down the clock, get Simone out of the house, and we'll be there to see who shows up?" Logan asked.

Quinn circled the room, wondering over to a table covered in pictures. "Yeah, I think running down the clock is the way to go. What is this?" His blood ran cold as his eyes took in a picture of him opening the door of Axis Management from Friday night.

"Yeah. Someone took those, maybe JayJay?" Nick said.

"Had to be," Quinn said. "Marion was on a cruise on Friday night. Axis Management has security cameras. Can we see if their cameras picked up anything on the street?"

"On it, there's just a lot of footage to go through," Nick said.

Quinn crumbled up the photos, wanting to smash his fist through the wall. "This is proof JayJay is behind this scheme. Do I trust what Gerald told me?"

Instantly, Quinn's chest grew tight, and his hands curled into fists as Erik strode into the room.

"Easy, man. He has a theory," Logan said.

"Don't want to hear it. He's not that smart." Quinn crossed his arms and glared.

Erik scoffed at him. "We think it connects to Marion because she's the one with the money. From everything we know, the lady has no reason to kill Simone," Logan said.

"Maybe she's pissed that Simone couldn't make the marriage work?" Quinn said.

"There's another option," Erik said

"Didn't ask you," Quinn spat the words out.

"You've got to hear him, brother," Logan said.

Quinn glared icily at Erik. The guy had balls.

Looking straight at him, Erik shoved aside Logan's arm as he tapped the photos on the table with his index finger.

"I think Carson, aka JayJay, is behind this all on his own," Erik said.

Quinn dismissed the theory with a snort.

"No. JayJay doesn't have any money, and why would he want to kill Simone?"

Quinn didn't want the bastard to be right, but he knew in his gut he had missed too many pieces of the puzzle.

"According to his social media posts, Marion fired him," Nick said.

"Being fired isn't motivation," Quinn said, grabbing his buzzing phone.

"Depends on how pissed off you are about it," Erik said.

"He gets fired and gets mad enough to set Marion's house on fire with Simone in it?" Quinn rubbed his hand over his face. "What did Simone ever do to Carson?"

"Yeah, it's fucked," Nick said.

"Quinn, you've gone soft. If it were me, I would have that sweet sub tied to the bedposts with a gag in her mouth until I found out who was out to kill her by fire," Logan said.

Quinn exhaled. He wanted to, but he didn't want to scare Simone, and he knew he was chickenshit by not taking that option. But it had been so long since he felt himself care about someone. He didn't want to risk scaring her, losing her forever because he went all mega Dom on her.

"I'm going to keep Simone safe, my way." His cell chirped, and he glanced at the screen. "Kayleigh, I'll call you back."

"Is this your idea of teaching me a lesson?" his sister shrieked at him.

Holding the phone away from his ear, Quinn tried for a deep breath. "Calm down. I can't understand-"

"You told me to keep up the writing! I can't do that if you scare off the people, I'm supposed to interview!"

"Kayleigh—"

"Simone stood me up! This is all your fault. You told her not to come! Didn't you?" Kayleigh yelled. Quinn's fists curled, his heart rate sped up.

"Got to go. I'll talk to you later."

"What's that about?" Logan asked.

"Simone agreed to meet Kayleigh for an interview, but she never showed up. That's not like her, something's happened. I got to go and find her."

"Wait, let me run a search for her car," Nick said. Nick typed furiously and brought up a surveillance program they used. "Do you know her plate number?"

Quinn strode over to the computer, punched in Simone's plate number.

Quinn paced back and forth, his heart hammering. What if JayJay thought to speed up the timeline and act now, where she was alone and unprotected? Damn it! He was an idiot for leaving her alone for even a moment.

"Quinn, there's an accident. It's Simone's car, just off the exit ramp."

"Fuck. I swear if anything's happened to her, I'll strangle both JayJay and Marion myself. Gotta go."

He bolted out the door, Logan on his heels.

"We'll keep watching here, but you have to admit Erik's theory has some legs."

"The deadline is tomorrow. Let's figure it out before then," Quinn said. "I've got to find Simone."

"Quinn, wait, let me come with you," Logan said.

Ignoring him, Quinn jumped into his truck and peeled away.

If only he had put a locator on Simone's phone. His head wasn't in the game. He was too worried about scaring Simone.

He'd let his guard down, rushed in too quickly, and now someone he cared about was in danger, and it was his fault again.

17

CHAPTER SEVENTEEN

Continuous beeping brought her to consciousness. Simone swallowed, her mouth gritty and her head foggy. Not even after a Create-a-Cocktail session had Simone ever felt this woozy. Beeping came from the curtained space next to her. Voices squawked over the intercom. Simone remembered a bevy of nurses and realized she must have fallen back to sleep. The disappointed expressions of the pair of police officers who took her statement flashed across her mind.

She wished she had stayed in that elevator with Quinn. God, her arm hurt. She wanted to call him. Her chest felt tight as she recalled the police officers talking about a dangerous driving charge. She couldn't tell Quinn about this, and she couldn't call him.

Simone's hands pressed hard into the mattress as panic speared through her. If they charged her, she could lose her job. And would that be so bad? The thought surprised her, but she wondered if she was cut out to be on television. She wanted something more.

She ran her hand through her hair, looked up at the splotchy tile, the panic easing as she thought about it. She had taken the job on the morning show because Marion told her to, and it was a distraction that helped her through each day when her marriage was ending. But it wasn't what she wanted.

The curtain swooshed open. The attending physician adjusted her glasses and peered at Simone.

"How are you feeling?"

"I'm fine." To prove it, she got up, her side and elbow aching, but put her feet on the floor.

"You have no concussion, no bruising, and we detected no alcohol in your bloodstream. You were lucky you didn't crash into the barrier. Follow-up next week with your regular doctor for the test results and don't drive when you are tired. You should call someone to take you home."

Simone bit her lip. She didn't have anyone to call. Marion wasn't home from her cruise yet, Meredith was on her honeymoon, and considering how angry Ava was, she didn't want to call her. She wanted to call Quinn.

"Thanks," Simone said to the doctor's back. Quinn would never fall asleep at the wheel. Her cheeks grew warm thinking of him, and she rubbed her hands over her face.

Simone took her jacket, grabbed her purse, and squinted at the bright lights of the hallway as she walked towards the exit, her body dragging with every step.

"Need a ride?" The steel in his voice made her belly flip-flop. His azure gaze roamed over her as if checking that she was in one piece, from her feet to her head.

"Why are you here?" She fervently wanted to wrap her arms around him, but she crossed them over her chest.

"To give you a ride." Quinn's firm grip scorched her arm, and he marched her out the door. "No concussion?"

"No. Not even a scratch. My arm is sore from wrenching hard on the wheel, but they said I'm fine."

"Good." Quinn's stormy expression was darker than usual.

"How did you find me?" She shielded her eyes from the setting sun, the ray of light highlighting the bottom half of Quinn's face. His lips pressed together, making his handsome features look sharp and unyielding.

"Get in." Quinn opened the door for her, and his icy stare made her squirm. "Are you mad at me?"

He crossed his arms over his chest. His icy glare could freeze the Sahara. "Why didn't you call me?"

She hadn't wanted to involve him. She figured she could go home, then meet up with him for dinner as planned. Simone stared at the concrete ground, her stomach in knots. Who fell asleep at the wheel?

"I didn't want to trouble you. I can call a cab." Simone looked down at the pavement.

He took two steps towards her and grabbed her chin.

"You're worth the trouble." His tongue darted in her mouth. He kissed her hard as if the suction of his lips could drive away his anger. She clung to him, his strength casting away her anxiety.

"When Kayleigh told me you didn't show up for your interview, I knew there had to be a good reason for you to skip out on it."

"I forgot about the interview." Kayleigh had been so kind and open to her.

Quinn wouldn't forget about an interview. He must be mad she skipped it.

"It's okay."

"No, it's not. I'll reschedule with her and invite her for a tour of the studio."

"I'm sure she would like that. Get in." Quinn opened the door for her and buckled her in.

"Thanks for coming to get me," Simone said.

"As I said, you're worth the trouble," Quinn said.

He didn't answer how he knew she was at the hospital and Simone didn't think he was going to tell her. So much for being open and honest, the flash of annoyance she felt surprised her. He came for her, she's happy he did. Simone chewed her lip, it's like his pointed control here, unsettled her As they drove out of the hospital parking lot, she texted Kayleigh an apology, adding lots of smiley faces and hearts.

"What happened?"

"I'm not sure. I was going to get a cup of coffee, and then my brain got foggy. I felt myself tilt. I veered left, stopped hard seconds before I hit the concrete barrier. They found me asleep at the wheel."

His shoulders hunched as he gripped the wheel hard. His usual stormy cloud was heavier. If it were anyone else, they would have fussed over her. That Quinn accepted her answer when she said she was okay made her feel like he truly listened. He skipped the flowery words and showed up.

"This isn't the way to my house. Where are we going?"

Quinn's palm on her thigh seared her through the soft material of her yoga pants.

"Simone, on Friday, I asked you to put yourself in my hands. Do that now. I'm going to take care of you."

Her chest tightened. He gave her no reason not to trust him. Everything he told her he came through on, but tomorrow he would leave.

"For tonight."

"Okay." His ability to read her mind annoyed her and stared out the window.

A few minutes later, Quinn pulled into the driveway of a small red-brick bungalow.

"What I know about you, Simone Roberts, is you like to be in control. It's your way of protecting yourself so you don't have to engage in the scary world and chance being rejected again. You convinced yourself the threats to your safety aren't real, so you don't have to deal with them. Am I warm?"

God, those blues pierced her depths, and he wasn't warm. He's standing in the fire.

Simone's head throbbed as he got out of the truck. Quinn knocked on the door, and a curly black-haired woman handed him a bag. Quinn waved and got back into the truck.

"Who was that?"

"Josie Agosti. Axis Management orders food from her, from time to time. She has a small catering business."

"You think of everything."

"I figured you hadn't eaten since this morning, and you mentioned you don't cook. I didn't think you had time to grocery shop between the wedding and how busy we've been."

His grim smile didn't reach his eyes.

He anticipated what was needed, and did what needed to be done. Her heart beat frantically in her chest. She wanted him to hold her, wanted to feel the warmth of his body like a blanket on a frigid night. She blew out a breath.

"You're right, but I went to the grocery store before going to Ava's—"

"You stopped for groceries, then went to Ava's?" His intense scrutiny made her fidget in the seat.

"I wanted to cook for you," Simone mumbled. Her face grew hot. She knew it was a silly idea.

"You were going to cook for me?"

The surprise in his voice made Simone tense up, and she hung onto the grip bar, afraid of having another accident.

"Yes. I had it all planned out. Then Ava asked me to get her make-up bag. I stopped by her place, and then I fell asleep at the wheel. Maybe I can't have marathon sex."

"Maybe you need more of it." He spat those words out, and she felt heat creep up her face. Simone glanced at him, finding his expression still set in stone.

At her house, Quinn came around the door, helped her up the steps, then slung the bag of food over his shoulder

Her hand trembled as she fished out her keys.

"I've got you." He took the key from her hand and unlocked the door.

In the wide halfway, Quinn hung up his jacket and held out a hand, steadying her as she slipped her shoes off.

Her honey hardwood floors glowed in the afternoon light. She watched Quinn as he took in the living room with its simple wide low white armchairs, the pops of yellow on the textured walls. He set the bag on the kitchen counter; his mouth curved up at the corners. Her heart fluttered.

"You tried to ignore the kitchen." He smiled.

She never thought of it before, but it's the only room she did in a dark colour palette, from the small navy island to the almost black cupboards.

"Nice garden." He strode over to the back door, pulled the door open.

"It's my favourite part of the house," Simone said.

He frowned as the door opened. "Simone, you must lock your doors."

God, the look he gave her could freeze the Sahara.

"I'll work on it. Quinn." She needed to say his name. She wanted his reassurance and as she did, her protective wall crumbled.

In two steps, he pulled her against the hard planes of his body, his arms came around her, his hand cupped the back of her neck.

"Eat, change, or bath first?"

"Need a quick shower, then change." She wanted her clothes off her. Her clothes carried the smell of the hospital.

"Your house is stunning." He walked through her bedroom, checking her windows.

"Thanks, I still think of it as Marion's. She has several properties and let us have this one, but she didn't sign it over to us because she gave Liam money for his business. She's been generous in letting me stay."

"I'm glad you have someone who cares about you." His voice sounded strangled.

This wasn't how she wanted to show him her bedroom.

Done in soft tones of lavender and grey, the largest room had a sitting area, a king bed, a vast window that overlooked her garden.

"I'll be out in ten?" Simone said, opening the door to the bathroom.

"Take your time. I'll get the food set up," Quinn said.

"Okay" She walked into her bathroom, startled when she caught his stormy expression so close behind her in the mirror.

"Simone..." He grabbed her arm and whirled her around then his lips crashed into hers, his hand came around her nape. "I want to do naughty things to you."

Tension in her body evaporated as he sucked and nipped at her bottom lip.

"What's wrong?" Quinn's thumb across her cheek swiped away a tear.

"I thought you were mad at me. I'm relieved you're not rejecting me," Simone said.

"Oh, baby, I couldn't reject you for all the gold in the world." He wrapped a few strands of hair around his finger.

"Okay." She placed her hand over his heart, feeling the thud against her palm. It made her feel connected. Gently, he removed her hand and kissed her on the forehead. He reached into the shower stall and started the water for her.

"Are you okay getting in?"

"Yes, I'll be out soon," Simone said.

"Take your time," Quinn said and left her along with the cool water washing over the scents of the day.

She wished he had stayed.

"Come, let me feed you," Quinn said.

He took her over to her breakfast nook. Simone fingered the cut roses on the small table, their leaves almost powdering. She watched him move around the kitchen, finding bowls and utensils.

He came for me. It made her heart swell.

"Here we are." He set a bowl of steaming soup in front of her, with a piece of crusty bread on a side plate.

Simone sipped the most wonderful soup.

"Oh, wow. This is good. How did they find this cater?"

"The Montague brothers know everyone. Why didn't you call me Simone?"

She fidgeted in the chair. "Who falls asleep at the wheel? It's embarrassing."

"That first night, when I told you to strip for me, you were embarrassed then, too?" His icy tone sent shivers along her spine.

"Yes." She flushed, grasping his point, remembering how he commented on her pride then, too.

"So you let your pride come before your safety? Your needs?"

"Quinn, I've looked after myself for years," she whispered. She stood on the brink of letting him in further to her tightly wrapped pain. She swallowed hard at the thought of him seeing her as weak.

"Submission is about leaving it all on the floor. It's about letting yourself be needy and vulnerable." He slid his knuckles over her cheek.

"Maybe I can't go that far. Maybe I should have kept it as a fantasy. You look after everyone, and you shouldn't have to look after me."

"You gave me your submission. It's my privilege to look after you. I made myself clear on this. I told you I expected you to ask for help when you needed it."

Her stomach tightened. "But Quinn, I didn't need help...." Simone kept her gaze on the soup bowl.

"You could have called me after you met with the police this morning. You could have called me after you left Ava's. And you should have called me to pick you up from the hospital."

Simone twirled the soup in her bowl, scooping some up then letting it drip off her spoon.

"Simone, I don't think you believe you are worthy of having someone care for you, of being kept safe."

She shifted on the seat, running her hands through the roses. The dried petals fell onto the table.

"You can't control life by ignoring your needs or by not engaging in living. I don't know why you lost control of the car. I have questions about how they handled the security for your father, but that wasn't your fault. And Simone, your husband being so detached that he couldn't even last through dinner before needing to leave the house? That is absolutely not your fault."

Tears pricked her eyes. She swept the rose petals from the table, letting them drop on the floor.

"You're running away by going on that fishing trip. You haven't mentioned if you're coming back, you talk about leaving as if it's final. You said you no longer work at Axis Management. What are your plans, Quinn?" She couldn't believe those words left her mouth.

The flash of pain across his face made her duck her head. "Fiona sold the house. I'm going to see it one last time, and to be honest, I haven't let myself think about what that means, but it's making Jordan's death more real. But you're right; since he died, I've done the same things I see in you. Until I saw you at the reception." His hand on her cheek spread warmth through her body. "Eat, then I'm going to tuck you in for a nap. What I want to do is take you to Club Bandit and give you that flogging."

"Just a flogging?"

"No. I want to punish you for not calling me." His steel tone blazed her.

"Do it." Her spoon clattered against the empty bowl. She pushed her chair back under the table. "I want to go to the club."

If he didn't come back from his fishing trip, she might never know if she could go further in her submission, and she wanted to find out.

"I'm feeling fine."

"No" He grabbed her arms, slamming her against his hard chest, his strong arms embraced her. "You need rest first."

"Are you going on your fishing trip tomorrow?"

"Yes."

"Then this might be the only time we have. Please, Quinn, I want this."

His warm hands scorched into her cheeks as he held her face, peering into her eyes. He kissed her hard and fast, a searing period to end the discussion.

"You're going to bed, Simone. Then later, if I'm convinced that you're really up to it, my flogger will caress your body in such a way, you'll wonder why you ever asked for it. Take some rest."

With his arm around her shoulders, he led her to her bedroom and pulled back her covers. "Baby, I have to call Zee to open Club Bandit for me. I'm not going anywhere right now. Rest."

"Okay. You win." Yawning, she got in bed.

He pulled the blankets over her and kissed her lips. "Good."

18
CHAPTER EIGHTEEN

W hile Simone slept, Quinn tided the dishes, swept her already clean floors, and paced. And when he couldn't take another back and forth from her front door to her back circuit, he opened her front door and made his way around her property, looking at her neighbour's half-wall of new brick. Damn it. He needed to solve this because if he cared about her at all, he would leave. He wouldn't take her to the club, no matter how she felt. He would pack up his truck and start the long drive cross-country to a small two-bedroom house, with vinyl siding and where the door never really closed properly. He rubbed his hands over his face. He should call Fiona.

Ignoring his own advice, he called his fellow Bandit Brother, Gabe, instead.

"Hey, Quinn," Gabe shouted over the whirring noise of a helicopter in the background.

"Bad time? I need to talk to you for a few."

"Hold on!" A moment later, Gabe came back on the line. "Sorry about that. I just landed. What's up?"

Surveying the street, Quinn strode through the back gate into a paradise of greenery. He quickly filled Gabe in on the situation with Simone.

"So what kind of drug wouldn't show up on a blood test they would run at the hospital?" Quinn asked.

"It could be a lot of things, but it sounds like a sleeping pill or an antihistamine. That's my best, not a doctor but merely a medic guess," Gabe said. "You have it bad for this girl."

And Quinn heard the wistfulness in Gabe's voice. He was a selfish asshole. Gabe had broken up with his long-time girlfriend and sub, Ivy, and while his breakup with Rachel didn't garner any remorse, Gabe's break-up had sent a ripple through their group. They had loved Ivy, and all felt betrayed by her, so if it were anyone else, he would have hedged.

"Yeah, man. I do. I'm going to take her to the club tonight. I still have no leads on who wants her dead, but her former mother-in-law is at the top of my list," Quinn said.

"That's fucked-up, man. Sorry, I'm not there for this one."

"Where are you, anyway?"

"On a job for Axis Management, leaving from the middle of nowhere. I'm taking all the work they throw at me. Grab a drink when I'm back there?"

"I'm heading home," Quinn said. His stomach dropped as he thought about his plan to go home, say his goodbyes, and never look back.

"You've got to do what you got to do. Good luck with this psycho, Quinn."

"Thanks, man, be safe," Quinn said.

Back inside, Simone was still sleeping. He'd just backed silently out of her bedroom when his phone buzzed. Quickly, he shut the door and answered.

"The money came from Carson Watson's account," Nick said. "Right into yours."

"Fuck, I was right," Quinn said.

"Why are you so sure it's Marion and not Carson on his own, like Erik said?" Nick asked.

"Because he doesn't have the money to do this all on his own. Thanks, Nick. I appreciate it. You guys trail Marion tomorrow, and Logan and I'll be nearby. If the people Marion hired are as amateur as we think, they'll be somewhere close."

"We should trail Carson, too."

"We're too thin. I would be surprised if Marion came near the house, but I want to know where she is when the attempted arson occurs."

"Okay, we'll do it your way," Nick clicked off.

Damn, things were heating up. And they'd been doing so ever since he laid eyes on Simone Roberts through a photo. Hearing running water, Quinn met Simone as she came out of the bathroom.

"Hi," she said.

She looked stunning there, standing at the side of the door, her hair loose and tousled over her shoulder, her nipples visible through her gauzy shirt.

"Hey, gorgeous." He brushed her lips with his, lightly, but it wasn't enough, and his tongue danced with hers, her taste flooding his senses, feeling just right and everything he didn't need. For a flickering moment, Quinn doubted his plan to leave. "How are you feeling?"

"Like I'm ready to go to Club Bandit." She grinned.

His little bird had stretched her wings. Damn, the woman was sexy as hell, and he couldn't say no to her. As her Dom, he should push her past her comfort zones, give her what she asked for, and explore her interests with her... His next breath stalled in his throat. Her Dom? Quinn ground his teeth. If only.

"All right, Simone. But remember, you're going to wish you hadn't asked me before the night is through," he whispered the words in her ear, saw the blush creep over her face, and kissed the back of her neck. "Let's get going."

"What do I wear?"

"It doesn't matter. I plan to keep you naked all night long. Pack some clothes for after, though." He stopped, noticing she ducked her head, looking at the floor. "Baby, what is it?"

"I want to dress up," she said. "And I have just the thing."

"Show me," he said.

Simone reached out, tugged at his hand. "Come with me."

He followed her behind her bed to a walk-in closet.

"You have some mad organization skills," Quinn said. He stared at the meticulously organized space. Clothes hung neatly on hangers, arranged by colour and fabric. Each pair of shoes had its own small platform. A make-up table with a mirror sat between two shelves.

"I use my house as practice for my clients sometimes," Simone said. "And one of my clients needed their own dressing room. I loved it so much I recreated it in my space."

"Every woman I know would love this." It was more than a closet. It was an entire organization system, custom-made to fit the space behind her bed, and Quinn admired her design skills.

"Thanks." She looked at him, blushed.

"What is it, Simone?"

"My sock drawer."

She pulled open a wide birch-coloured drawer and stepped aside.

Quinn peered in. On top, there was a synthetic flogger, a thin crop, a pair of fuzzy handcuffs, a stack of envelopes, and a folded piece of purple fabric.

"So, every time I tried something, if it was a salsa dancing class, tickets for a couple's spa or the flogger and Liam said no, I tucked it in here. I've never shown it to anyone."

His eyes misted, and suddenly he had a hard time swallowing. This was an intimately wounded part of herself, and she'd shown it to him. He pulled her close, wrapped her in his arms, and kissed the top of her head.

"Damn, Simone, I'm so sorry." Sorry that her ex was a douche, that he couldn't honour and love and protect her like he had promised her. And equally sorry that he couldn't fill that role when it came down to it

"It's all right," Simone said. "But I was wondering if I might wear this?" She went to the drawer and pulled out the folded-up piece of purple fabric, revealing a corset trimmed in black lace.

"Yes! I want to see that on you, at least for five minutes," Quinn said.

Simone's laughter rang out, easing the twisted knot in his heart. "I'll be ready in ten?"

"Yes, and not a moment longer. Throw some clothes in a bag in case we stay the night." He kissed her hard, tugging at her bottom lip, felt her shudder and let go, slapping her on the behind. "Go."

***

Zee and Ella Ridell met them at the doors of Club Bandit. Quinn introduced Simone, and a deep pink blush settled in her cheeks. "Welcome to Club Bandit. It's nice to meet you," Zee said.

Ella took her hands in hers. "If you need anything, please let me know."

"Thanks for opening her up for me, Zee," Quinn said.

"Anything for you," Zee said. "It's nice to see you out. You two enjoy yourselves, and you know where to find me."

Zee opened the doors to the club for them, the lights switching on as he pressed buttons on a wall panel.

"Have fun!" Ella waved, and the couple turned right to the stairs to their private residence.

"Thanks."

Simone gaped at the waterfall wall behind the small desk

"This is beautiful."

"They did a great job with the place," Quinn said.

Deep in his wounded psyche, more of the grief and the hurt knitted together, his pain healing, as Quinn watched the rapt expressions on Simone's face. He wanted to give her so many new experiences. She reached out, ran her hand along the bronzed textured wall, walked past each play station, taking in the various pieces of equipment at each one. She touched the leather spanking bench, frowned at the pole cemented in the floor, and at the last corner, she stopped where a medical table with the fasteners hanging from various points was displayed in the half-light.

"You like that?" Quinn leaned in and whispered in her ear.

"I'm intrigued."

He laughed as he felt her body shiver.

"Were you expecting dark and grimy?"

"Yes," Simone admitted. "But this makes me think of an old-world European living room," she said, putting her hand on the back of a Victorian chair as he led her through the sitting area off to the side of the bar. She blushed, noticing the oversized cushions on the floor.

"I love the spotlights under each station," Simone said. "It's warm and light."

"Play areas need to be well lit so the Top can see what they are doing. Zee and Ella have put a ton of thought into this place."

"People know about it?"

"It's open to an exclusive few, but there's talk of that changing." Quinn guided her through the room with his hand in the small of her back. "This way."

As they walked down a curved staircase, Simone ran her hand on the smooth stone handrail. "I can't believe this place," she said, her voice tinged with awe. "Thanks for bringing me here."

Damn, his heart was going to burst.

Quinn stopped outside of the third door down. "This one is my favourite." He punched in a code on a panel next to the door. The green light flashed, and he gestured for Simone to go ahead of him.

The floor here was hardwood, polished to a sheen. The room was sparse, with a sink and a bar fridge on one side, a shelf that held bacteria wipes, a box of condoms and a blanket, and an armless chair against the wall. Simone's eyes grew wide, as she took in the only other thing in the room, the ring hanging from the ceiling.

He couldn't wait to play with his pretty submissive. Simone clutched her hands in front of her, glanced behind her shoulder at the door.

"I got you. And it's up to you how far we go, Simone. Say, 'red' and we stop. You can leave at any time." Taking her hand, he pulled her against him, slanting his lips against hers, he could feel her racing heart as he tasted her. His fingers tangled in her hair and he broke off the kiss, tracing her swollen lips.

"How are you feeling?"

"Fine."

Shaking his head at her, Quinn took her chin in his thumb and index finger. "Fine, is not an acceptable answer. You need to communicate and tell me everything you are feeling."

"I'm nervous but eager to get on with it." Simone flashed him a smile.

Quinn tilted her face to him. "Baby, you're going to strip for me and kneel under that hook in the ceiling." Her indrawn gasp sent the blood rushing to his cock. He pulled her close to him, his hand squeezing her breasts under the silky material of her corset.

"Yes, Quinn."

He smacked her on the ass and undid the strays on her corset. Damn, she looked so sensuous, so gorgeous, and she was his. For tonight, she was his.

Quinn strode across the room, set his leather bag and Simone's pink one, and sat on the high-back chair, watching as she let the corset fall, folded it, and placed it on the shelf by the door. Her kitten heels came next, then her black skirt that barely covered her thighs, then her shimmery nylons.

She glanced over at him, and Quinn gave her a nod. Like she had been kneeling for her Dom forever, she gracefully squared herself under the hanging hook, fell to her knees, then lowered herself more, so her forehead was resting on her hands. Damn. He wanted to ravage this woman, make her scream for him, and never let her go.

19

CHAPTER NINETEEN

Fuck, what a perfect picture of submission she made. Simone's honey hair shimmered under the soft light; her breasts touched the hardwood floor, subtly rising and falling with each indrawn breath of hers. And as he made her wait, her breathing became deeper, like she was finding peace the further she allowed herself to let go. He forced himself to relax, crossing his feet at the ankles, his hands at his sides. He wanted Simone to feel a sense of anticipation. He wanted her to feel his eyes roaming every inch of her smooth, pale, naked skin as she stayed in position on the hard floor. But it took a lot of his willpower to stay in the chair. He wanted to race across the room, spread her wide, and sink into her lava core like a frustrated pent-up virgin.

But he could wait.

Being here with her was pure medicine to his wounds, and he wanted to soak it all in, faintly hoping it would last beyond when he had to leave.

After a moment, he reached into his leather bag, pulled out lube and a plug, and then his favourite smooth paddle; heavy and made of maple, the wrapped handle smooth against his palm. He strode with determination across the room to her.

For a moment, it tempted him to have her lick his boots, have her clasp the back of his calves, have her fingers work his zipper open. But tonight, it was about her.

He rested a hand on her head, and one shuddering exhale from her pillowy mouth, singled to him the reassurance she found under his touch.

He swallowed, flooded with the visceral memory of how much touch served as the vehicle of communication. Tonight, through his touch, Quinn wanted to convey to her how much she meant to him, and he wanted her to feel worthy of attention and care and having her desires fulfilled.

"So beautiful, kneeling here waiting for my touch, for my command." Quinn slid his hand up her back to her nape, splaying it wide open between her shoulder blades. With firm but soft pressure, he pressed down, so she raised that beautiful ass of hers high in the air. "Spread your ass cheeks for me."

"Okay," her voice was breathless.

He applied pressure to his touch. "Yes, who, Simone? Who am I tonight?"

"Sir," Simone said.

"That's right," Quinn kissed her between her shoulder blades.

"Very nice," Quinn said. He glided a hand along her spine, down to her luscious ass. Quinn crouched down beside her, grabbing her chin in his fingers. "You've given me your submission, Simone. But tonight, I want your surrender. I'm going to push you, but I'll catch you when you shatter." Quinn kissed her. The sweet taste of her sparked his desire.

"I want this. I want you."

Damn, her voice thick and gravely sent his cock throbbing.

"I want to exceed your fantasies, Simone, and send you flying back into subspace." His hands caressed her cheeks, her neck, slid down to her bottom. "I want to make you feel so cared about, you never doubt it again." Damn, his voice choked up, but he got the words out. Moving behind her, he rubbed circles on each of her round globes, circling her rosebud, then dipping a finger lower, reaching her warm folds. Her pussy nearly suctioned his fingers right in.

She mewled, and he withdrew his finger, wiping it on her ass. From his shirt pocket, he took out the lube, spread a good amount in his palm, then spread her ass cheeks, his fingers digging into her sensitive skin, and from the same pocket, he took out the plug.

"You remember this, don't you?"

She cried out as he circled the plug around her rosebud. "Tonight, I'm going to take you there. Arch towards me, baby." Her body easily took the plug. He kissed the base of her spine, feeling her shudder under the touch of his lips.

The sight of her, plugged and ready, filled him with pride. Damn this woman with her sweet innocence and her willingness to trust him. The logical part of his brain that told him it would be better if he stopped this, got in his truck, and drove away, quieted. He couldn't turn away.

He gently tapped the base of the plug with his favourite paddle. She swayed under it in surprise.

"Stay still," Quinn said. "What do you say if this becomes too much?" he slowly dragged the paddle over her ass, as if it was another hand caressing her.

"Red," Simone said, her voice husky with need.

"That's right. I'm going to bring this paddle down on your ass six times, and you're going to count and not move. Is that clear, Simone?"

"Yes Quinn…" she breathed out.

Standing, he walked around her in a slow circle, thumping the paddle against his leg. "Good girls… say what they want."

With a flick of his wrist, he swung the paddle through the air, bringing it straight across both butt cheeks.

Simone yelped, bringing her legs under her.

Quinn pressed down on her back. "What number was that?"

"One." Her eyes met his, widening, a hint of defiance, he wondered, or the need for reassurance? Quinn stroked her hair, felt her relax.

"Which means we have five more. Get back in position."

Simone blew out a breath, then sank down, spreading her knees.

Satisfied, Quinn strode behind her, sailing the paddle through the air and bringing it down on the centre of her left ass cheek.

Simone yelped. "Two."

Quinn flipped the paddle in his hand. He dragged the edge of the handle along her side, over her pink spots.

Simone hissed.

"Good girls… ask for comfort." Quinn brought the paddle down hard on the underside of her ass cheeks, Simone shrieked, his hand came down hard, on her hip holding in place. "Breathe, you're fine, and I've got you."

"Three." She spat out the word. Her nutmeg eyes flashed at him.

He chuckled. "We'll get there, baby. You're still thinking, trying to muscle your way through this. But you have to give it up, Simone. "

He whooshed the paddle through the air and pulled back, halting the force, but brought it down hard on her sit spot.

"God!" Simone panted. "Four."

Quinn placed his hand on her shoulder, waited until her breathing returned to even, and she stretched out her knees back out in place.

Striding around her, hitting the paddle against his hand, Quinn's mouth got dry looking at her. "Good girls… ask for help." With an overhand swing, he brought the paddle down on the pink spot on her ass with another thwack and then another.

"Five, six," Simone whispered.

He set the paddle on the shelf behind him. Crouching down in front of her, he trailed his fingers over her soft cheeks, wiping away a tear. He sat on the floor and brought her into his arms; then he kissed her hungrily.

"You took that punishment so well, Simone. Good girl."

In his arms, she heaved a sigh, put her arms around his neck, and turned her head so it was against his shoulder.

"Thank you, Quinn."

His heartstrings hauled. He kissed her forehead, brushing his hand through her hair.

Slowly, he guided her to standing. Turning her around, he took out the plug.

"Hey!" Simone cried.

"Did you want me to leave it in?" Quinn's mouth quirked.

"No, Sir," Simone muttered.

At the sink, he washed his hands and passed her a bottle of water from the fridge.

The smile she gave him made desire pulse at the base of his spine.

She melted the cage of icy grief around his heart and took up space, and he couldn't shake her if he tried.

"Can you hold me?"

His arms encircled her, bringing her small body hard to his chest. She fit perfectly.

"I want to hold you forever, Simone, but my cock is so hard it could drill concrete. I want to be buried balls deep in you."

She wiggled against him, her bare red ass against his hard erection. Reaching between her legs, he fingered her folds, putting an arm around her chest. This is how he liked her, leaning on him for support, opening to him under his touch. He nuzzled her neck, biting her gently between her shoulder and collarbone.

"Damn it, girl, I can't get enough of you."

20

CHAPTER TWENTY

"God." The low moan escaped her lips, and she closed her eyes as his jeans abraded her smarting ass. His fingers pumped in and out of her, and Simone arched towards him, wanting him to ease her aching need. Wanting him to take her into that blissful place he had shown her was possible.

"But first that flogging." His rough hands on her cheeks caused her eyes to open, meeting his lapis orbs. This man pulled her into his depths, and she wanted to stay there.

"Quinn." She needed to say his name, her fingers reaching up to feel his whiskered skin. No matter what he asked her to do, she would... because of him. She felt seen and at peace in a way she didn't know she needed. Trust. The realization gripped her, but instead of making her want to bolt, it was a warm brand of comfort. She trusted Quinn.

"Stand under the ring."

Walking across the room, Simone could feel the heat of his stare, and her nipples beaded. Wetness gathered between her thighs and trickled down her legs. Her stomach coiled in a knot of anticipation—it was becoming a familiar sensation, and the excitement coursed through her veins.

Quinn smiled. Her breath caught in her throat as he strode toward her, with the length of black rope in his hands. He circled her. She stood there, her hands clasped in front.

"Gorgeous."

Her entire skin was aflame at his touch. He took her hands, stretching them up above her head to the overhead ring, curling her fingers around the cool metal. Then he slowly tied her forearms together. With every pass of the rope, Simone's body pulsed in anticipation.

"So sexy," Quinn murmured.

Simone moaned low in her throat as he kissed her abdomen, her thighs, landing a soft kiss above her mound. She arched towards his face with her hips, and he slapped her thigh.

"Hey," she said.

"Patience," he grinned. "Is this what you want, Simone? To shut off the world and let someone else take control?"

She swallowed hard, meeting his piercing glare. "No. I need *you*, Quinn, to take control. Not just someone."

God, where did this bravado come from? It was Quinn that made her feel brave. Quinn made her feel free enough to voice her needs.

He cupped her face in his hands, tilting her chin to him. His mouth crashed into hers. Quinn's woodsy scent filled her nostrils. His fingers pinching her nipple made her moan. He swallowed her sounds as his hand moved to the other breast.

She pulled at the secure bonds, wanting more of his touch, but he shook his head at her, a small smile playing around his lips. Walking to the other side of the room, Simone held her breath as he reached into the leather bag. He pulled out a flogger, snapping its tails against his legs as he walked towards her. Simone clenched her legs as he slid the tails slowly around her shoulders, around her breasts and torso. The strands felt buttery soft.

"This is a soft deerskin flogger. A warm-up. How does it feel?"

"Good." There was a haze behind her eyelids. Quinn strode a few feet in front of her. Simone hissed as he brought his arm back, and the strands of the flogger whooshed through the air, landing on her lower abdomen.

The stripe of deerskin crashed through the hot sensations on her skin.

"More."

"You got it," Quinn said.

He walked behind her, the flogger hitting the backs of her calves, striking her buttocks, her shoulders, over and over in some intricate pattern, and as each stroke landed, her body went slack, hanging there from the metal ring. She made whimpering noises over and over.

"Now you're warmed up." He kissed her hard. Her eyes fluttered open, and she smiled.

Returning the deerskin flogger to his bag, he switched it for a black-handled one.

"This one will sting." With a flick of his wrist, the strands of the flogger landed above her hip.

God, the bite of pain it left as Quinn threw it left, then right, left again. A sense of amazement rose within her. The bolt of pleasure, making her feel boneless. Her breathing became shallower, her head lolled. He had to continue. She mewled, cried out, and moaned because it seemed to urge him on every time she did, and the flogger came down on her skin with a snap.

"Simone."

He pressed his thumb on her clit. "You're soaked."

The pride in his voice made her heart bloom. She tried to meet his eyes but felt so laden she couldn't lift her gaze.

"Yes, more."

"I'm going to flog your breasts."

In response, she thrust them out to her as far as the slack in the rope allowed.

"So beautiful."

Standing back, he threw the flogger through the air. The moment the tail landed across her breasts, her eyes flew open in startled surprise, and she jerked forward.

"Yes! Thank you, Quinn."

As the flogger came down on her breasts, Simone felt waves of pleasure crash into her. Her vision blurred, it became too hard to keep her eyes open and she relaxed against the bonds, listening to the flogger slap her skin. The pain and pleasure warred with each other, until it all mounted into a blaze of intensity and burst of rolling rapture.

When she felt Quinn's hand on the back of her neck, she opened her eyes.

Trailing the flogger over her nipples, Quinn kissed her collarbone, then lowered his mouth to her breasts that he had just flogged. "You are so damn sexy."

He kissed her and fingered her clit as his tongue danced with hers.

She whimpered.

Taking his fingers out of her pussy, he put them to her mouth.

"Open. Taste how wet you are."

She did, savouring her saltiness, recognizing her need, and remembering how 'out there' she had once thought this was when Quinn first made her taste herself on his fingers. Now, she licked them with fervour. He plunged his fingers in and out of her mouth, fast and furious, and she leaned forward, sucking them so hard her cheeks hollowed.

"Good girl."

He pulled his fingers out and brushed his knuckles over her cheek.

She whimpered against his touch.

"You're floating, girl," he said, his voice thick with emotion. His warm hands massaged her arms, massaged her calves, and suddenly she was out of the ropes, falling forward into his hard chest.

"Thank you," Simone whispered.

He took them down a set of stairs. Lights flicked on as they walked under the motion sensors. At the second door, he stopped and punched in a code on a panel by the ball.

This room was all muted blue on the walls and a big four-poster bed, clean white sheets, and fluffy pillows.

He set her down gently on the soft surface.

"This place is full of surprises," Simone mumbled.

"You should see the upstairs. Drink."

He held a bottle of water to her lips.

She drank it down almost in one gulp then fell back onto the bed.

After he undressed, he slid into bed next to Simone, taking her in his arms.

Never had she felt so connected to herself, so aware of her desires. She arched into him, taking his hand and placing it on her abdomen.

"What do you want?" Quinn asked. His voice was thick with desire.

"You, Quinn," Simone said.

Trailing his fingers along her neck, over her breasts, down the plane of her abdomen, Simone arched to him under his touch.

His touch was ignition, making her burn with need as he kissed her lips until they felt swollen, as he kissed her collarbone, between her breasts, down her stomach. She could lose herself in him.

The look he gave her seared her, and she knew this wasn't a good idea. He'd said he was going to leave. But right here and now, she didn't care.

He pushed her down gently, grabbed a condom from the nightstand, and rolled it on.

Moving down the length of her, he dropped soft feathery kisses along her torso.

"Open and show me where you want my mouth," Quinn demanded, his voice heavy with need.

She spread her legs, tapped her clit with a finger. "Right here."

"Damn it, woman." He put her legs over his shoulders, his hands grabbed her smarting ass cheeks, and he titled her hips to his face.

She dug her fingers into his shoulders as his tongue went right to her clit. God. She was flying somewhere in a world of hot sensations and need. His tongue twirled around her clit. He sucked and nipped, and Simone moaned, felt herself tighten, the release almost there, and he withdrew, bringing her legs down gently.

"Cruel man." She reached for him.

"I can be," Quinn agreed, "but it's going to be worth it. You spread so well for my toy. Now turn over and spread for my cock, Simone."

21
CHAPTER TWENTY-ONE

Her lips pouted, and he laughed. Damn, she had come a long way. His chest swelled, loving how open she was with him. He loved her trust in him; he didn't deserve it, but he was going to soak in it, cement this moment in his memory. Right now, at this moment, he was going to give her another new experience.

With a glance over her shoulder, she did as he'd ordered and spread her ass cheeks. Quinn grabbed a pillow, pushed it under her hips. Gliding his hand over her ass, he growled. Her rosy cheeks had a red stripe from his lash, and he bent, nipping it gently.

He grabbed the lube from the nightstand, coated his sheathed cock, and then plunged his finger into her channel. Her smooth skin bumped his thighs as she writhed under him. He slapped her ass and sawed his fingers in her tight, scorching passage.

"You like that?"

"Yes, Quinn." Her voice, whiskey-laced, urged him on. Her hands fisted in the sheets.

"I'm going to make this so good for you, Simone." His voice broke on the words. He said it with devotion. The only promise he could offer her. He kissed the back of her neck. Her light gasps of pleasure made his cock throb. He slid another finger in, deep.

"Ride my fingers, Simone," Quinn gritted out.

His little bird did, arching her hips higher, gyrating on his fingers, moaning low in her throat.

"God, Quinn, I need you."

Easing his fingers out of her passage, he turned her head, kissing her perfect lips so hard they swelled. "I've got you, Simone."

He stroked his cock, and slowly slid the tip around her tight hole, making a slow circle. Simone arched, wiggling her ass.

"Bear down on me, Simone. Breathe out. That's it," Quinn said. He slid out again and back in. Oh, so slowly, he thought he was going to explode with the effort. His balls drew up, and tingles drummed at the base of his spine.

With one thrust, he slid past her tight ring into her tunnel. Damn, she was so hot around his cock, so tight. As he plunged into her again, Simone whimpered. Reaching around her waist, he dove his fingers into her wet folds, and he circled her clit with his thumb as her heat gripped his throbbing cock. Her pussy clamped around his fingers. Quinn gritted his teeth, wanting to hold out.

"Quinn," Simone panted out his name, and he wanted to hear her voice, thready filled with desire voice every damn day. This woman undid him. One more thrust brought him balls deep, buried in her inferno.

Circling her clit, he rocked deep inside her. The heat of her consumed him, making the edges of his vision black.

"Come with me, Simone!" Her pleasure was all that mattered to him. He wanted her to come undone. She tightened around his fingers, and an electric current ran from the base of his spine to his balls.

He rocked his hips and drilled right into that hot centre, her walls tightening around him as the orgasm took her under.

"Yes!" Simone cried out. "Quinn"

And with his name on her lips, he plunged into her, once, twice, and once more, exploding into her heat.

As she shuddered with aftershocks, he pulled out of her hot channel. He brushed her sweaty hair off her shoulder, kissed the back of her neck.

"Quinn," Simone said, her voice breathless. "I love you."

As if he had been punched, Quinn sucked in a breath, pulled away from her, and sat on the edge of the bed.

"Quinn, you wanted me to be honest." Her hands rubbed his back as if trying to reassure him. He should reassure her. But he couldn't. Her words re-formed the wall of ice around his heart. This plan of his was a bad idea.

He shook off her touch. He threw the condom in the bin in the bathroom, washed his hands, and splashed his face with cold water.

Those words she'd said weren't true, but a part of him wanted them to be.

She probably wanted him to say something back to her. Quinn shook himself and went back into the bedroom to find Simone curled on her side.

He brushed his hand over her hair. Damn, she looked so soft and vulnerable. Her forest floored eyes met his, and damn, his girl was brave.

His girl... if only.

"Simone." Her name, the only word he had. Damn, he hated himself.

His phone buzzed, and he practically leapt off the bed for it, then frowned as he read the screen.

It was another reminder that the last three days couldn't last. The text read: "Deadline almost up. You have until 2:00 pm."

"Fuck."

If things were different, if he had something to offer her, a family, a home, if he wasn't so wounded, maybe it could be more. But he had nothing to offer this woman, and she deserved someone steady and dependable, someone without wounds.

He had to treat this as if it were a job. He couldn't give Simone what she needed, what she deserved, but he would do everything possible to keep her safe.

22

CHAPTER TWENTY-TWO

Maybe it was the unfamiliar place or the sky lightening to grey tones that caused Simone to wake. As her eyes opened, she snuggled down in the blankets and smiled. It was another night spent with Quinn, and though it was the last thing she'd expected to happen, she wouldn't want it any other way. She peeled off the covers, noticing an achiness in her body, and then the last moments came back to mind. Her stomach dropped to the floor. She ran into the bathroom. Her hair was a mess, her skin flushed, a faint mark of Quinn's fingertips along her collarbone. She splashed cold water on her face

So much for being the woman who didn't make mistakes. She had made a big one by saying that little four-letter word.

Staring into the mirror, she shook her head at herself. Quinn had told her from the beginning that he didn't do long-term commitments.

But she had fallen in love anyway, not doing a thing to stop it.

Her breasts were red and rosy, a bite mark stood out on her shoulder. Simone turned the shower on and let the warm water cleanse some of the soreness away. Maybe he'd gone to get coffee. Maybe he'd needed to answer his cell or make a call. Simone closed her eyes under the spray of water. His hand had brushed her hair, his finger had paused on her lips. Then he'd tucked the blanket around her, and she had fallen asleep.

But he must have come back.

Wrapping a towel around herself, she took an unopened toothbrush from the basket of toiletries and brushed her teeth, and combed her hair.

She closed her eyes tightly as reality came crashing into her brain. She had to be at the studio this morning.

Back in the room, she looked for his leather bag and didn't see it anywhere. But her pink bag was on the bench at the end of the bed. She was alone.

From her bag, she put on a pair of leggings and a light pink dress. Looking at herself in the mirror, Simone shook her head. She had blazers at work she could toss on over the dress and back up clothes if this washed her out under the lights. But her cheeks had a rosy colour, her lips swollen from Quinn's kisses, and her body still sore from his cock.

God, what had she done?

Gave herself over to him. She'd given him everything she had, and he'd made her feel cared about. He'd made her feel adored.

Until she'd vomited those words out.

She grabbed her bag and her purse and opened the door.

Her heart began to beat fast as she stepped into the corridor, trying to remember which way was out from last night. As she walked, security lights blinked on, and she found a door. As soon as her hand touched the doorknob, she jumped back as flashing lights and a high pitch alarm split the air.

And that was the tipping point for her simmering emotions. She fell to the floor, digging through her purse for her phone, tears threatening to spill.

"Hey."

At the rough voice, Simone looked up to see a man with short-cropped hair and thick muscles looking down at her.

"I tried to open the door."

"I can see that. Where is Quinn?"

Trying to keep herself from crying had been too much effort. Tears spilled over, and sobs burst from her throat.

"Hey, you're fine," said the stranger. "The noise will stop in a moment."

Simone shook her hand, swiping at her face as hot tears fell on her fingers.

He tapped in a few numbers on his phone, and within minutes later, the red-haired woman Simone had met the night before came running.

She wrapped Simone in her arms.

"Oh, honey, let's go sit outside. Thanks, Erik."

Pushing through the double doors, Ella took Simone's hand in hers and sat her down on a wicker chair.

Simone gulped in the cool air, and if it were under any other circumstance, she would have admired the expansive garden.

Dawn had just lit the sky in the early hour, washing the garden in hues of pink.

"I can't believe he left," Simone said.

"You have every reason to feel wretched right now, and I won't defend Quinn. Leaving you like that was an awful thing to do. But I've known him for a long time, and he had to have had a reason."

To her utter embarrassment, Simone put her head on her arms and cried her heart out. Ella patted her back, making soothing noises. It was a long moment before she stopped crying.

"Whatever the reason, it isn't acceptable that he left you," Zee said, coming to join them.

He set a tray of tea and fruit and toast down. Simone shivered.

Zee poured her tea. The tiny cups looked ridiculous in his hands, but he also appeared to have done this a thousand times.

Ella opened a cedar chest, took out a throw blanket, and settled it around Simone's shoulders.

"Did you play last night?" Zee asked.

Shaking her head, Simone clutched the blanket around her. She didn't know these people.

"I own a BDSM Club, and there isn't anything I haven't heard or seen," Zee said. His smile warmed up his features, making him look a lot less intimidating.

"Or done," Ella added, her eyes twinkling.

"All of this is new to me," Simone said, waving her hand towards the club. "He is the first man I confessed to about having fantasies, and he made one come true. And then I screwed up."

As she tried to stop the tears, her hands started shaking, and Simone closed her eyes tightly.

"Him leaving you is not your fault, Simone," Zee said. He covered her shaking hands with his, and she nodded.

"It hurts. It shouldn't. I only just met him, and I know it was my fault he ran."

"It's not your fault. Quinn has demons he battles," Ella said.

"He's an asshole," Zee said.

Simone shook her head, trying to stop crying.

"He told me he doesn't do commitments. Last night, I told him..." She couldn't get the words out.

Ella wrapped her in a hug, and Zee bore into her with a serious stare. Simone looked down at the ground.

"The lifestyle is not a fantasy. Doms are human too, and they can hurt you. I apologize for this happening under our roof. I thought Quinn was ready, or I wouldn't have agreed to let him have the space privately."

Ella encouraged her to eat. After taking a few bites, Simone felt better. Zee asked her what she needed.

"I have to get to work on time," she said.

Not that she felt like it, but she wanted to get back to her life.

Ella offered to drive her, and having no other choice, Simone accepted. She worried she was going to have to make conversation until Ella flipped the radio to bad country music and her trying to sing along to it made Simone laugh.

Before Simone exited the car, Ella passed her a card with Club Bandit's logo on it.

"My cell number. Call me anytime."

Simone knew she wouldn't call her. She didn't want any reminders of Quinn.

Squaring her shoulders and plastering a smile on her face, Simone pushed through the doors of the studio.

She had a job to do.

"Good morning, Simone, you're here early," Henry said.

"Got to get back to it," Simone said.

Giving the security guard a wave, she stopped to talk to Paula at reception, asking about her sister.

"She's almost off the crutches," Paula said, twirling her brown hair.

"How was the wedding?"

Meredith's wedding felt so long ago, the question jarred Simone out of her thoughts.

"It was great! Meredith was so beautiful, the whole thing went smoothly."

"She's a lucky woman," Paula said.

"Yeah."

She wished Meredith was here right now. She would pour her heart out to her about Quinn. Meredith would know what she should do.

While waiting on a single-serve brew in the kitchen, Simone checked her phone.

He hadn't even texted her.

Blinking back tears, Simone fixed her coffee and took it with her into the tiny room she used as an office.

It relieved her when, moments later, Meghan knocked on the door. Simone drank down her coffee, took a deep breath and smiled.

Following the make-up assistant into the dressing room, Simone began to feel better. This was routine; this was what she did. All she had to do was get through the next few hours, and then she would go home and eat a lot of chocolate and hide under the blankets forever.

"Do you need anything? You look a little pale," Meghan said, waiting for Simone to climb into the make-up chair.

Under the bright lights of the dressing room, her skin looked as tired as she felt.

"Just a bottle of water, thanks."

"I'll go grab it and be right back," Meghan said.

Simone leaned forward, rubbing her temples. This morning's segment was on fall decor, and she needed to pull herself together. She needed this job, if only for her sanity.

But did she *want* this job? Simone bit her lip. She had realized how much she didn't want to be an on-the-air designer in the hospital.

Simone tried to gather her thoughts as she waited for Meghan. The memory of Quinn's words in her ear, his hands on her waist, his whiskered cheek against hers flooded her mind. Opening her eyes, she shook her head, trying to clear the memory but her body remembered with the aches she felt, her flush still warmed by the imprints of his touch. She had never felt more like herself, more at ease. The longer Quinn went without contacting her, the more apparent she had scared him off for good in that single moment of truth.

If she was being honest with herself, she had loved Quinn since first setting eyes on him. He made her feel cherished and safe and more than that; he brought out a confidence in her that made it okay for her to be feisty. Simone didn't think she had that kind of confidence, at least not after her marriage to Liam and the confidence it sucked out of her, a confidence that was restored by having this job. Leaving this job would be a mistake.

Closing her eyes, she leaned back in the chair for a moment, running through the script in her head. When Marion had first told her about the opening here, Simone hadn't been sure, but when she came in for an audition and realized it was like talking to her clients, she felt comfortable and took it. It had been the lifeline she needed. But now, she wanted something different.

Quinn.

"Here, Simone," Meghan said, coming back into the room. "You're a little early, but we can get started now if you like."

"Thanks," Simone said, a sip of water, clearing her head. "Where's Ava—?" Her ringing cell phone cut her off, and she rummaged in her bag, trying to find it.

"Hello, Marion" She had been holding off on taking her former mother-in-law's calls long enough and as overbearing as the woman could be, Simone still loved her and wanted to hear a friendly voice.

"Darling, where have you been? I needed a few more things from the attic, and I couldn't find my backup keys. Can I come by later?"

"I was out," Simone said, her face blushing at thinking where exactly she had been, entangled in the sheets with male muscle and glorious sex. "I'll text you when I'm done here."

"Okay, see you soon," Marion said. "Good luck with your segment. I'll be watching!"

Simone hung up the phone and sighed.

"All ready to go?" Meghan asked. The assistant make-up artist stood by her with a sponge in hand.

"Shouldn't we wait for Ava?"

As annoyed as she felt with Ava, considering what had happened last night, it looked like her friend was right.

"You didn't know? Roger fired Ava on Thursday."

She shook her head slowly, feeling gutted.

"No, she didn't mention it throughout Meredith's wedding."

"I heard she threw a fit and security had to escort her out," Meghan said, dabbing moisturizer on Simone's face. "Poor thing. She's so talented, but her attitude is going to affect her in this industry."

Despite her loyalty to her friend, Simone had often felt the same thing. Ava was quick to show her temper and fits of jealousy.

"Awful timing," Simone muttered. That explained Ava's behaviour at the wedding, the excessive drinking and her distant attitude when Simone brought over her make-up case.

"Definitely. It must be hard having such a famous sister," Meghan said.

"I couldn't imagine."

Closing her eyes, she let Meghan do her work and tried to calm her thoughts. She felt like a lousy friend, not realizing all that Ava was going through. No wonder she wasn't the nicest to her on Saturday. The first person she wanted to talk this through with was Quinn, and she felt tears well up in the corners of her eyes as she realized that wasn't a possibility.

After every line was in place, Simone was ready to go on camera. Walking on set under the bright lights, she got that buzz she always did when she was about to do her segment. Simone took her place behind a faux marble counter, held up a basket of apples and candles.

"As we say goodbye to summer this weekend, I thought I would show you some quick and easy fall decorations you can make yourself easily at home. Fall is an entire season, more than Halloween, so today, I'll show you how to make a sunflower wreath and an apple candle holder."

As she went through the motions and did her demo, falling back on her script, the tension left her, and she could stay in this moment and pretend last night hadn't happened.

As soon as her segment was over, and they were on to commercial break, Simone got off set quickly. She wanted to go home, put on her comfiest PJs and sit in her garden with a hot chocolate.

"Simone, Roger is on his way down to talk to you," Francie, the production assistant, said.

"Okay," she flashed her a smile but groaned inside. Conversations with her boss were never quick. Oh well, she knew she had a change of clothes in the small office, and she would curl up on the sofa until he got down here.

Simone gasped, as an iron grip reached around her wrist, yanking her into the office. Her throat went dry, her heart pumping in overtime.

She put her hand on the door and found herself hauled against corded muscles. Shock rippled through her as she met the glacial blue stare. "Quinn."

23
CHAPTER TWENTY-THREE

Her umber eyes darted back and forth, anywhere but meeting his gaze. Her hand reached for the doorknob. He took her hand in his, instead.

"Simone, about last night—"

"No. I don't want to talk about it. You left." Her voice quivered on the word. His heart ached. He wanted to give her reassurances and declare how he felt about her on a jumbo screen, but he couldn't. It wouldn't be fair to her.

"I did. But I'm here now. I didn't leave you." His voice broke, and he didn't care. He was desperate.

"Are you cancelling your trip home?"

The rise in her voice, the hopeful note, sliced through him like a steel blade. "No."

"Then why are you here? Didn't you take enough from me?"

Oh, his little bird was showing her backbone.

Quinn ran his hand through her hair. He felt a little out of his mind. And that was why he'd had to see her. "I don't know. Did you give me everything?"

In a second, his mouth was on hers, his hand around her waist, pulling her close. His knee came between her legs, pinning her against the door.

"Quinn, I can't—"

But her body softened against his, and he drove on, his tongue dominating hers.

"Damn it. Ever since Jordan, my head has been so fucked up. I wish it were different. I wish it hadn't happened. I wish I could stay for you."

As her lower lip wobbled and tears leaked down her face, he wiped them away.

"Come away with me, Simone."

"Quinn—" She pushed back from him.

He sat down heavily on the black sofa.

"I thought I could keep you safe, but I can't. You need to get security."

Damn, he'd said too much; he stopped talking, ran his hands through his hair.

"Quinn." Simone's voice was barely above a whisper. "Do you want to tell me what happened to Jordan?"

He glanced at her face.

It had that open look of compassion. Her tears, he realized, weren't for the hurt she was feeling. It was for the pain she knew he was feeling.

In one smooth move, she came over to him, taking his hands in her soft small ones. She kneeled in between his legs.

"You can tell me."

He swallowed past the lump in this throat.

"Baby, it's better if I don't."

"I want to know. I can take it," Simone said.

Her big brown eyes bore into him as if she could see past the walls he kept.

He was leaving anyway, and it wasn't just his story. He should tell someone before he disappeared forever.

"We tracked Mulberry's kidnappers to the Basin Desert. Our helicopter dropped. I was going to run into the tent, along with Gabe and Nick. Logan, Jordan, and Erik were behind us, Logan and Jordan to look for whoever took Mulberry, and Erik was scanning. I got into the tent first and saw Mulberry tied to a stake in the ground. I got to work freeing her."

He closed his eyes, remembering the scared, bone-thin woman he had found, how she had dry heaved when he freed her ankle.

Simone's soft touch on his hands kept him anchored to the present.

Wanting the rest of the story out, he continued. "Gabe checked her over for injuries, and Nick was standing at the door of the tent. Nick heard it first, another helicopter. Erik should have found it before it landed. I left Mulberry with Gabe and Nick and ran out to see the helicopter had landed. It was firing at our helicopter and the next thing we knew, an explosive went off. I ran right in through the dust and smoke, but Jordan was down. Logan pulled me out. We grabbed Mulberry and got out of there. I left him, Simone."

His throat was scratchy and dry, his cheeks were wet.

"Quinn, I'm so sorry you lost Jordan, but it's not your fault." Her warm hands on his forearms soothed him, and he wished he could fall into all the softness he knew her to be, but he couldn't.

"It is my fault. When it's your op, you're responsible for getting everyone out and alive. What does everyone think of me now? I'd resigned, planned to go home and say goodbye, and then I met you."

He pulled her up and kissed her, her luscious berry lips soft, her eyes filled with tears.

Maybe now she would understand why he couldn't be with her anyone, why he couldn't have a relationship, not with his demons. She slid her hands up his forearms, her touch warm and wonderful, her gaze filled with—

He shook off her touch. He didn't want her pity. "Come with me now, and I'll make everything right." He pulled her in tight to his chest.

A knock sounded on her door.

"Quinn, I can't just leave."

Her voice was heavy with regret. He let go of her before he threw her over his shoulder and hauled her out of this building and into his truck and then out of this city. His hands brushed her hair. He reached into his pocket and pressed an embossed card with Axis Management's logo on it.

"Take this. It's a direct line to Xander. If you need them for security or anything, they'll cover you. Take care of you. Goodbye, Simone."

"Quinn, you don't have to go," Simone said.

Quinn turned around. Another knock came on the door, and it opened. A tall man with dark brown hair strode in, clutching a tablet.

"Simone, good to see you." The man leaned in and gave her a peck on the cheek.

With one glance back, Quinn left.

On his way out of the building, his phone buzzed. Logan, wondering where he was. He had just told her goodbye, but that didn't mean that he didn't want to finish this job, which would be his last. Then he would get in his truck, say goodbye to his mom and Fiona, and take it from there. He wasn't sure what there was. Maybe he would disappear, work light security somewhere, maybe some mindless warehouse guarding job. Maybe he would flip burgers. Quinn laughed, the pain in his chest making it hard to breathe. But first, he could do this one last thing for Simone.

***

In record time, he made it to Simone's neighbourhood.

Quinn squinted in the bright afternoon sun. His head pounded, and his skin felt dry and tight. If this is what knocking back half a bottle of expensive whiskey did, he was damned relieved that it wasn't a habit he'd developed. Throwing on his sunglasses, he shoved his hands in his pockets and walked past Simone's backyard. At her neighbour's, a large German shepherd barked. He looked at the ground, observed the other people on the street. A man across the street was cutting his grass, a neighbour across the street and two doors down was painting an awning. At the end of the street, the sound of wood slapping against the plastic street hockey ball pierced the quiet.

He wished he could take back what he had done last night. Bolting on Simone was the worst response to her confession. Any trust he'd gained, he had thrown it all away. And then showing up at her work to dump his pain on her. If she didn't regret saying those words earlier, she definitely did now.

Those three words wrapped around his heart like a vice, and if he didn't leave, he knew he was going to explode. Or say them back to her, and that couldn't happen. He wasn't the guy to have a relationship with.

He promised to keep her safe, and he was going to do that even if he made it harder on himself.

Quinn ran over to the white panel van that was parked across the street from Simone's house.

Sliding open the door, he barked out, "Anything?"

Logan shook his head at him. "All quiet. No sighting of Marion or JayJay. I don't know, Quinn."

"It has to be Marion. Whoever she hired is going to be here to finish the job."

He glanced at his phone, muting it.

It was Zee, calling again, to give him a piece of his mind.

Logan grinned and shook his head at him. "It's fine to give a woman what she wants, but a Dom gives her what she needs."

Logan's words hit their mark, and Quinn winced. His friend was right. Every time he got close to pushing Simone, he backtracked because he wasn't ready to be vulnerable.

In the back of his mind, Quinn thought if he could gain Simone's trust, she would tell him everything about her life, and that would lead him to whoever was out to cause her harm. It hadn't worked. He let his emotions get in the way. He fell hard for Simone, being more concerned with not scaring her and fulfilling her fantasies than actually keeping her safe. It felt good to give someone something. He didn't want to put in the work required for a relationship with boundaries; he didn't trust the Dom/sub relationship.

"It was a better plan in my head," Quinn admitted.

"I think Rachel did a number on you," Logan said, echoing his thoughts.

Rachel was a brat who had delighted in goading him, but truthfully he wasn't in the place for a relationship. He wasn't interested in chasing; he wanted a relationship that gave, and Simone gave him more than he'd ever expected.

"Lady has taken her dog to the groomers, had coffee with a friend, and is now getting her nails done." Erik's voice echoed through the van, making Quinn want to punch the door.

"It doesn't take a criminal mastermind to pay someone. She has the money."

Drumming his fingers on the door, Quinn knew the excuse sounded flimsy even to him.

"Hello," Logan said.

Leaning forward, he watched as Simone's friend Ava got out of a car, walked up the steps, and sat down on the porch. She ran her hands through her hair as if trying to make it messy, pulled out her phone, and then started crying.

"Who is that?" Logan asked.

"Simone's best friend."

His stomach dropped. He had barely glanced at Ava because she *was* Simone's friend, and when he'd met her at the wedding, she hadn't struck him as a person who had it together. He brought up the photo of the ring found the night of the brick being thrown. When Erik sent him the picture, he had discarded it, not giving it much thought. The ring was two bands of silver, and he rubbed his upper arm, remembering how the prongs around the rubies felt when they scratched his left biceps as he was helping to steady the drunk woman.

Logan snapped a few pictures of Ava from the car and ran them through a search engine.

"She's Meredith Philips' sister. She would have money."

"I don't know. Simone seems close to her," Logan said.

Logan snapped his fingers. "She looked familiar. My neighbour is a key grip at the studio, and he told me about this contest."

"What are you talking about?"

He wondered where Simone was. If she were home, Ava would have rung the door. He wondered how Ava knew she wasn't home, and he cursed himself all over again for running out on her last night. And for leaving her at the studio. He should have stayed with her.

"It was a huge thing last year. The morning show ran this reality TV show type contest because they had a spot to film. They cancelled it suddenly. It was fresh news because it upset a lot of the contestants, including Ava, who got a lot of press from it because of being Meredith's sister."

Quinn ran his hand through his hair, frustrated. "So petty jealousy is behind this?"

"It's as good a motivation as anything."

Quinn watched Ava check her phone again.

"Lady seems to be on her way in your direction." Erik broke the silence.

"I'm going out," Quinn said, his hand on the door.

"She's met you, and Simone isn't here yet. Wait," Logan cautioned.

Huffing, he cooled his jets. His friend was right.

Scrolling on his phone, he brought up Ava's social media, trying to find a connection between her and JayJay Harris.

"She won't see me, but I have to get out of here. Keep looking for a link between Ava and JayJay."

"All right. Keep your phone on vibrate and answer me if I ring," Logan said.

Quinn rapped his knuckles on the roof of the van and hopped out.

He kept watch, making sure hedges covered him and hoping the neighbours weren't peeping out of their windows.

As a car turned onto the street, he walked over to the neighbours on the left, taking cover in the hedge.

24

CHAPTER TWENTY-FOUR

Simone rested her head against the window of the cab as it turned into her neighbourhood. Tomorrow, she would get her car out of impound. But between her falling asleep at the wheel and the brick being thrown at the windshield, half of her wanted to stick to Ubers and cabs.

She shifted her shoulders. Her body still ached from being with Quinn, only reminding her of all she'd enjoyed at Club Bandit and all that hadn't worked out. She couldn't get Quinn's face, tight with tension, out of her mind. She didn't think she would ever forget how his voice rang with pain as he'd told her what had happened with Jordan. He hadn't sounded like the confident Dominant she knew.

Over the last three days, he'd fulfilled so many of her fantasies and given her pleasure, which she hadn't known was possible. But her heart twisted at the emptiness of it. She wished she could accept it for what it was: three unbelievably epic, sexually charged days. But her heart didn't want to move on.

His pain wasn't the whole of the man. He'd shown her such care, tenderness, and trust. She'd never experienced loving attention like that, but maybe he was just being a good Dom. That was what dominants did, show care and tenderness to their submissive. She'd taken it for something more. She wanted to forgive him for leaving her at the club, especially since she knew she shouldn't have said those three little words. This wasn't supposed to be anything more than an extended one-night stand. He had gently taken her through the things she wanted and pushed her to accept more.

She shifted in her seat, trying to find a more comfortable position. Her ass was still tender from his paddle, her body languid from the flogging, and she felt used all over.

Used.

Her heart felt used, even if her body felt satisfied. No matter how much she told herself, Quinn didn't mean to hurt her. She could only blame herself. She consented to everything. Said yes to everything and now she longed for what couldn't be.

She blushed, remembering the feel of his cock in her ass. How she wished she'd clamped her mouth closed on that "I love you."

The cabbie pulled into her driveway, and all thoughts of huddling in bed disappeared as Simone spotted Ava sitting on her step.

She paid the fare and rushed over to her friend, noticing how Ava's body shook.

"What's wrong?" Simone laid her hand on Ava's shoulder, and her friend shrugged it off.

"I'm never good enough," Ava said.

"That's not true! With your talent, you could do anything." Simone pulled her friend into a hug.

"No, you don't understand."

Seeing her friend so distressed sent a wave of guilt through Simone. She'd been so distracted; no wonder Ava wasn't her usual self when Simone dropped off her make-up bag.

"Come in." Simone held the door open for Ava.

"I guess you heard they fired me?" Ava looked out the window.

"Yes. Meghan told me."

"The studio likes her better than me. Everyone always picks someone else."

"You're a great make-up artist, and you'll find work quickly," Simone said.

"I doubt it," Ava said. She stiffened. "What's Marion doing here?"

"I know you two don't get along but she's only here for a minute," Simone said, frowning at the odd excitement in Ava's voice.

"I don't think I can take her," Ava muttered.

"I'll do everything I can to get her to leave," Simone said.

Pasting a smile on her face, Simone greeted her mother-in-law.

"Hello, darling," Marion said. Fizzy, Marion's white lap dog, barked and squirmed in her arms.

"Do you want to go right to the attic, to get the box you need?" Simone said, wanting both her guests to leave as quickly as possible.

"I want to catch up with you first!" Marion said. "And have a cup of tea."

"Of course. Ava is here too, and she's a little upset." Simone closed the door behind them.

"Good, she can tell me about the wedding!" Marion gushed, setting Fizzy down. "Hello, Ava!"

"I can tell you about it later," Simone said. "Marion, I'm happy to see you, but I'm feeling tired. Can you grab the box tomorrow night, and we can have dinner?"

"No time like the present." Marion sat on the couch while Ava paced back and forth, looking out the window, and Simone wondered what was up with her friend. Ava didn't like Simone's mother-in-law, but she usually wasn't this unsettled by her.

"Darling, your segment was just okay today. I wondered if you got enough sleep because you didn't seem as peppy as usual."

Flames licked at her face as Simone muttered about not sleeping very well these days. Her stomach sank, thinking again how her time with Quinn was over.

"You'll try, won't you?" Marion asked.

"Try what?" Simone asked carefully as she stepped over Fizzy and put the kettle on.

"Remember the chiropractor I told you about? He's done wonders for my sleep. I'll send you his number right now." Marion pulled her phone out of her handbag, shooing Fizzy's nose out of the way.

"Simone, make Ava a cup of tea. She needs it," Marion said.

"I don't need tea," Ava said, crossing her arms.

"You look a mess. A cup of tea will help," Marion said.

Seeing how jittery Ava was, Simone thought of Quinn asking her if anyone was upset with her.

Ava definitely was upset. But with her or the studio? Or with Marion being here? Simone shook the thoughts off, promising herself to schedule a girls' night out with Ava soon.

"Tell me, Ava, how was the wedding?"

"Perfect. It had to be. Everything is perfect for Meredith." Ava spat the words out.

"When you only get married once, it has to be perfect," Marion said. She fixed Simone with a knowing look. "If you were to get remarried, I wouldn't mind, you know."

"How lucky for you," Ava intoned. "You do nothing without someone's approval, do you?"

Simone blinked. That comment stung, and if Ava hadn't been her rock this past year, she would have told her to get out of her house.

The tea kettle whistled, and Simone took a deep breath as she poured water over the tea bag. She didn't want them here, and she wished she could tell them to go. She wondered what Quinn would tell her to do.

"Ava, you'll get a new job," Simone said, passing Marion her tea.

Fizzy yipped, ran frantically to the back door then back to Marion again.

"Fizzy, calm down. I'll take you out in a minute," Marion said.

Simone turned to see Ava shooting her a look. "I'm sorry, I shouldn't have said anything."

"Everyone knows about the firing," Marion said, waving a hand dismissively.

"Of course they do," Ava said, crossing her arms and glaring at Marion.

"Well, when you post videos of the anchors and make fun of them, there are consequences." Marion scooped Fizzy up. The dog spun out of her grasp.

"I wasn't making fun of them!" Ava yelled. "I was showing how their make-up could be better, but nobody ever listens to me!" She threw her teacup across the room.

Fizzy kept barking. Marion reached down and scooped up the dog again. "Ava!" Marion screeched.

"Ava, what's going on with you?" Simone cried.

"You don't get it! Nobody helps me. You ruined everything!" Ava gripped Simone's arm, her nails digging into her skin.

"Ava! Let go of me!" Simone tried to nudge her way out of her friend's hold.

"Calm down, Ava," Marion said, but she was by the back door, reaching into her purse, grabbing Fizzy by one hand.

"This was your fault, too! You just walked into the studio and gave her the job. If it wasn't for her, I would have the spot on TV!"

Marion screamed, Fizzy barked, and Simone swallowed. Her mind was whirring, and then Ava pressed a knife blade to her neck. The air whooshed out of her lungs. Where had the knife even come from? But it was there, pressed against her throat. God, this couldn't be happening.

"Ava! What are you talking about? Let go of her!" Marion said.

"The contest for the morning spot! I would have won that, but it got cancelled because you sold the producer a fuckin' house!" Ava shrieked and gripped tighter on Simone, the blade pressed into her neck. Simone gasped for air, trying to stomp on Ava's foot. What was her friend doing?

"Ava, the reality contest wasn't getting good ratings! I suggested Simone, but it wasn't her fault. If you were dependable, you would have a job!" Marion said.

"Everyone gets second chances except me and JayJay!"

"Carson? How do you know Carson?!"

"I met him at the comedy club. You fired him. We were going to move to LA to start over, but you ruined his reputation too!"

"He stole thousands of dollars from me!" Marion said.

"He's only going to get what you owe him. You never gave him that signing bonus you promised him."

Oh, God. Simone couldn't believe this was happening. Marion's face went ashen, and she shrieked as a man in a clown wig walked in through the back door.

God, why hadn't she locked her doors?

Simone closed her eyes, trying to elbow and twist out of Ava's grip, wondering why Carson, Marion's assistant, was wearing a wig. Ava's hold tightened on her, and Simone's mouth went dry.

"Ava, you're going to let go of Simone right now."

Quinn.

Ava jerked Simone around, and there was Quinn at her front door.

"Simone, you run when I tell you," Quinn said.

"We tried to get you to quit, Simone. Even drugging you didn't work. We paid lover-boy over there to set your house on fire, but if you want something done right, you got to do it yourself." Simone's heart was in her mouth. She blinked at Carson as he reached into his pocket.

"Carson!" Marion screeched.

Ava tossed Simone to the ground and ran over to JayJay.

From his pocket, Carson took out a black slender tube and lit it. Quinn launched himself through the air as a loud boom tore through the air. Simone screeched, heard Marion screaming, and felt all the air leave her body as Quinn covered her—for the third time in their history.

Pieces of her house splintered, and flames licked the walls.

Simone closed her eyes against the burst of light and shattering glass.

"Come on, Ava!" JayJay screamed.

"Simone, we got to get out of here!" Quinn said in her ear. "Simone!" he called his arms around her. He threw her over his shoulder, running with her through the garden. The edge of her vision grew fuzzy.

"Simone."

She didn't want to open her eyes. Her head pounded somewhere.

"Hey," Quinn said.

He had a cut on the side of his ear, and he was wincing.

"I need to... Where's Marion?"

"She's okay. Logan pulled her and the dog out. They're taking her to the hospital to get checked. You should go too."

"My house is burning." Simone stared, shocked at the flames licking up the outside of her house, at the smoke. Somehow, she was across the street. "What did Ava mean about hiring you?"

"Simone, let them check you out. We can talk about this later," Quinn said, putting a hand on her cheek. Simone pushed his arm away from him.

"No. Tell me, Quinn."

"I was trying to protect you," Quinn said.

"They *paid* you to set my house on fire? That's why you slept with me?" Was that her voice sounding so shrill? She closed her eyes, not being able to wrap her head around this information. "Why would you sleep with me if they hired you to kill me?" She shook with fear, with tension.

"I was mistaken for someone else," he said, running his finger along her jawline. "I was trying to keep you safe."

She pushed his hand off her, shaking her head.

"You didn't tell me I was in danger," she whispered.

Her heart shattered. She couldn't believe this was happening. Her house was in flames. The man she had placed all her trust in had betrayed her, and her best friend had betrayed her. Simone wrapped her arms around herself.

"You wouldn't believe me. I kept you close until I could figure out who was after you," Quinn said.

Simone averted her gaze, backing away from him. "You manipulated me."

He reached out to stroke her hair, and she jerked back.

"By having sex with me."

He closed his eyes briefly, and her heart lurched. Three incredible, mind-blowing days of sex and intimacy of being cared for, and it hadn't been real.

"By getting close to you," Quinn said. He shook his head, reaching out for her hand. "I did what I thought was best to keep you safe."

Looking at her destroyed house, Simone shook her head at him. "It didn't work," she said.

Her body was shaking. She clutched her stomach, feeling nauseous. Quinn took two steps towards her, and she held up her hand.

"Stay away from me."

"Simone, I can explain," Quinn said.

"Get away from me. You're a monster." Her voice shook, but she didn't want him to see her come undone. Even though he already had.

Fire trucks and an ambulance pulled up on the street, the flashing lights casting Quinn's face in a blue glow. He looked as hollowed out and as hurt as she was on the inside.

"Simone—" She heard the pain in Quinn's voice and steeled herself to it, turning away as the paramedics ran over to them.

She never wanted to see Quinn Walsh again.

25

—·—

CHAPTER TWENTY-FIVE

"You're a dumb-ass for driving," Logan said.

As Quinn reached for a folded pile of laundry, he winced as the fabric of his T-shirt chafed at his sore back, where the heat from the flames had scorched him.

"I need to clear my head, and I like my truck."

The ringing buzzer cut Logan's speech short, and he rushed over to answer his door.

Throwing his bag on his shoulder, he took one last look around Logan's modern open concept condo; he knew Simone would have adored it; Logan hid the TV behind panelling, and there were two abstracts by Deirdre on his friend's wall. He wondered what she would think of the stripper pole in the corner. He had to get out of here, being in this condo, in this city. It was making him miss her too much.

"You know, I might get a house out of this." Logan put the giant basket of fruit on the counter, and Quinn shook his head.

"Just happy you were there."

The moment JayJay had thrown an M-80 through the front of Simone's house, Logan had run to the back and got there just as it exploded. His friend had pulled Marion and her dog out to safety as Quinn ran out with Simone.

Ever since the attack, Logan had received something daily from Marion.

"I keep thinking of how we would have done this differently if it was a job."

Logan threw Quinn a kiwi and an apple and followed it up with a banana.

"Hey!" Quinn caught the fruit.

"It would have been different if you approached Simone from the beginning with what you knew. We would have operated with the client. Keeping secrets always leads to trouble."

Logan's tone of voice turned cutting, and Quinn raised his eyebrows at his friend.

"You needed to go full out Dom on her."

Quinn bristled at Logan's biting remarks. It had been Quinn who had taken his friend to his first BDSM Club, Quinn who had introduced him to kink, and it irked him that Logan was criticizing him. It irked him more that his friend was right and echoed his thoughts.

"I know. You said it before."

And he hated the fact that he would not get another chance. He bit the inside of his cheek. He knew he wouldn't see her smile, or the adoration in her eyes, or the flush on her face as he brought another ounce of pleasure out of her.

"You like this girl. Don't give up," Logan said.

"I'll call you when I get home. Thanks for everything, bro." Quinn clasped Logan's extended arm, and the big guy brought him in for a bear hug.

"Be nice to Deirdre, Quinn. And keep trying with Simone. Send her flowers or fruit. Keep texting her."

"I'm out of here," Quinn said.

Pausing on the sidewalk, he checked his phone. No new messages. He wanted to text Simone, but what would he say? *I'm sorry.* Spotting a jewelry store a few doors down, Quinn stared in the window. Never had he gifted a woman jewelry. But never had a woman got into his head, captured his heart.

He couldn't help thinking how the elegant gold strand would look around Simone's neck. Twenty minutes later, he had bought the necklace, making arrangements for it to be delivered to her door. As if they were back in high school, Quinn got Simone's location by having Logan ask Marion. It relieved him to know she was safe, staying at a bungalow in the suburbs.

He silently waved bye to Simone, climbed in his truck, and drove.

When he knew he was pushing it, he pulled over to a motel, got four hours of sleep, and did it all again the next day.

But even the Canadian highway wasn't long enough to keep his mind from thinking about the woman with honey blonde hair and soulful, big brown eyes. Thinking about her made his heart twist, but he didn't want to forget the feel of her in his arms, how she tasted on his tongue, her soft vanilla and peach scent. The way her eyes brightened with her smile. Simone might hate him, but she was safe, and that was why he'd got involved.

In his mind, he kept seeing the hurtful expression on Simone's face. He couldn't forgive himself for not figuring out it was Ava and JayJay behind the attack.

For Simone to tell him, "I love you," and then the very next night to call him a "monster" and not hear him out proved she didn't love him. That was what he told himself, anyway.

And it was a knife to his heart, hearing those words from her kissable lips, seeing the flash of pain on her face. Knowing he was the source of that pain.

For him, being a Dom, being part of the BDSM community, was a part of him. And open communication was a huge part of that. So he hated that he'd lied to her, no matter how he justified it. He should have told her about being hired to kill her. He breathed through his nose, clutching the steering wheel. When his phone buzzed with his sister's number, he ignored it. He loved his sister, but she always said the most thoughtless things to him. His parents screamed at each other, but somehow, they stuck it out. Quinn ran his hand through his hair.

Simone's world had just shattered. Quinn knew he got off pretty lightly. There were a lot worse words that she could have said. He was trying to protect himself by telling himself she didn't love him. He knew she did.

And maybe love wasn't for him. He was better sticking to play partners. Quinn snorted. That hadn't worked out either.

Maybe it was because love was for those who had stability, like a childhood home to which they could bring their loved ones back.

He couldn't picture classy Simone in the neighbourhood he'd grown up in, with the dated houses. Turning onto that street, he smiled. It was home.

On a quiet dead-end street, the blue bungalow looked perkier than it had in years. Someone had fixed the old railing that surrounded the porch. The cardboard and plastic covering the broken pane in the sunroom's window that Jordan had broken with a baseball when they were kids had been replaced with actual glass. The plants still sat on stacks of old books and hung off whatever hook they could find. The door to the shed was no longer leaning on the side, but straight up, and Quinn could almost smell the fresh coat of paint from here.

He faced combat; he faced life and death situations, but this was a whole different level of terror that coursed through his veins and made his hands palms sweat.

Not wanting to think about it for a moment longer, he forced himself out of his truck. Gravel crunched under his foot.

He tapped once, twice, three times on the window above the screen before he let himself in, wiped his boots, and walked up the three steps and into the kitchen.

Seeing the boxes on the floor, he ran a hand over his stubble, looking out at the backyard. It was true what they said. You couldn't go home again.

"Are you just going to stand there, or are you going to put on the kettle?" Fiona's merry voice rang out from the hall.

Despite himself, his cheeks hurt from the enormous smile across his face.

Quinn filled the kettle with cold water, got down the glass teapot from the shelf, along with the jar of black tea leaves.

"Well, it took you long enough," Fiona said, coming into the kitchen, a pile of books in her hands.

"Yeah, well, I'm here now." His voice caught in his throat.

Fiona threw the books in an empty box and stood in front of him. She had to look a long way up at him, but it always felt as if she was the taller person. He hugged his five-foot-nothing second mother.

"I heard you were moving."

"Finally, time for me to do something else. Going down to Boston to stay with my sister."

"You two will paint the town."

A small smile played on Fiona's mouth.

"You'll come to visit?"

"Yes."

"Good," Fiona nodded. She deftly took the almost whistling kettle off, poured the water into the teapot, and gestured at the kitchen table.

"You have time off work?"

"September is a good time for fishing."

Fiona tilted her head, gave him that look he knew so well. He sat down at the old wooden table, watching her.

"I'm not sure I want to work for Axis Management," he admitted softly.

Fiona raised an eyebrow at him. "What have you been doing instead?"

"Trying to help someone. It could have gone better."

"You always think that. If you weren't such a perfectionist, you would have an ego problem. Oh, wait."

Quinn grinned back at her and shook his head. "I failed to see the threat quickly enough. I missed the signs until it was too late."

"Is the person safe?"

"Yes."

"Then you did your job."

"I could have done better."

"Sometimes, it's not up to you."

Quinn sighed, watching her puttering around from fridge to counter. A nurse by profession, Fiona was always moving. A light dusting of white coloured her red hair. Otherwise, she hadn't looked like she aged at all. But there was wariness over her that wasn't there before, and he knew he had caused that because Jordan didn't come home.

"You know why it's not the same with Axis Management?" Fiona asked.

"Tell me," Quinn said.

"This outfit means something to you. You want to work there."

Shifting in his chair, Quinn snorted. But he knew it was true. Axis Management had given the five of them life after the service. Those Bandit Brothers had put a lot of faith and trust in his team, and they were his family.

"Jordan would tell me I was being a pussy."

"He would have been right," Fiona said, placing a plate in front of him.

With an arm around her waist, he pulled her tight and hugged her. "I'm so sorry."

"I know you are. He made his choices, too," Fiona said. She gestured to the plate. "Eat."

Quinn took a bite of the roast beef sandwich and shook his head.

"Damn, that's good. What else is up with you?"

Fiona sat down across from him, spinning her teacup in her hands, back and forth.

"I read Mulberry is in Vancouver again," Fiona said.

"Yes, for some kind of product launch. Xander asked me to be on the team, but I skipped out on the head shrink appointment, so...."

"You avoided it. Her mother writes to me," Fiona said. She pulled out the chair and sat beside him.

"She's a decent woman, despite the fame."

"I don't blame anyone," Fiona murmured. "Including you."

"Then you're a better woman than I am," Quinn's mouth quirked. Only because of her, had he turned out half decent.

Fiona smiled. "If this were a movie, I would give you his dog tags."

"That he never wore and never got jacked up for, the bastard," Quinn shook his head.

Fiona smiled at him, her expression sorrowful. After a moment she smiled, leaned forward in her chair.

"Tell me about the girl you rescued that has you so scared you drove home." Fiona looked into her teacup, smiling.

"She's wholesome and good, and I don't deserve her. She's not the usual girl I hook up with, not the type of girl I can bring home," Quinn said.

"Why not?" Fiona asked, raising her eyebrows.

"She had a normal upbringing. I mean, she had a cook and probably someone to clean. Her dad was a surgeon, and her mother a CFO. She's successful."

"She sounds like a bore. I didn't think money mattered to you." Fiona raised an eyebrow.

"It's just different. How do I explain all of this?" Quinn gestures around him.

"You have let go of the shame you felt about your mother. She loves you so much," Fiona said.

Quinn scoffed. Yeah, when she remembered to.

"Quinn, if you love this girl, then she won't care how you grew up or that your mother has a mental illness. She'll see home the way you do. The problem is, you're ashamed."

"It's not normal," Quinn said.

He shook his head. He knew he was stubborn by clinging to an image of perfection that didn't exist, and maybe it was shallow, but he couldn't let it go.

"Your mother could have felt insulted. She could have fought me. Instead, she recognized that you and Kayleigh staying with us was the best thing for you to do when she was trying to get herself sorted out. You think I saved you from care. But she did because if she or your father had fought it, who knows what would have happened? Do you think it was easy for her to know you two preferred being here, even when she evened out? But she never once said no to either of you when you wanted to stay here." Fiona levelled her wise look at him, the one that made him feel nine again.

"Sometimes we would wake up, and she would be here at breakfast," Quinn mused. He hadn't thought of how hard it must have been for his mother. He'd always thought Deirdre was happy to have them out of her way, even when she was on the level.

"Yes, because she loved you and missed you. You might not think it was normal, but you had love here and a street where everyone knew your name. I don't know what you feel you've been missing," Fiona said.

Quinn shook his head. He didn't know.

"I think you are angry at your mother for something she couldn't control and did her best with," Fiona said. "And I think it's time for you to let that go, get this girl, and be happy."

"That simple, huh?" Quinn said.

Reaching out a hand and putting it on his, those green eyes reminding him of his best friend, Fiona shook her head. "Yes."

"Okay then," Quinn said.

He wasn't sure how he was going to get Simone, wasn't sure if she would listen to him or give him the time of day, but he wanted to, he wanted to fight for her. She deserved someone who would fight for her, and dammit, he wanted to be that someone for her. He wanted to be the man she saw when she looked at him. The man she deserved to be with.

"I have something for you." Fiona got up, went to the front room, rummaging in her purse.

"Here." she put down an old key on the table in front of him.

Quinn picked it up, turning it over in his hands. "What am I going to do with two?"

"I don't know, but he would want you to have it," Fiona said.

"Better than a dog tag." Quinn grinned.

"One more thing, while you're here," Fiona said, her voice softening.

"I'm listening."

"Don't give Kayleigh that money. She needs to figure herself out, too. It's enough that you help her out with rent."

"Has she asked you?" Quinn asked.

Fiona nodded, clearing the teacups.

"I told her I would always be here for her, but I think she could explore going to college, at least taking a class or two, and she really should find an investor because it would be better business sense long term because it's going to take more money than she thinks to get it off the ground."

"How did she take that?" Quinn asked.

"She yelled at me and hung up, then called back an hour later, apologizing. You need to let her see if she can do this," Fiona said.

"I don't want her to suffer," Quinn said.

"Working hard for something isn't suffering. If she is really serious about this, let her see if she can do it," Fiona said.

"You make good points. Simone is going to like you."

"So that's her name." Fiona smiled at him, her eyes twinkling.

"Yeah. I think I've put it off long enough, don't you think?"

"Probably. Dinner tomorrow?" Fiona said.

Standing up, he pushed his chair in, took two steps across the small kitchen, and wrapped Fiona in another bear hug.

"Tomorrow."

"I'm counting on it," she told him.

Leaving his truck in the driveway, Quinn went over to the house with the red pickup.

The last time he had seen his parents had been at the funeral. His father had clapped a hand on his back, said, "He was like my son," and his mother had hugged him hard.

She had a trip to go on for her art right after. He hadn't spent time with her, but looking back, he realized she had looked healthier, looked the way she did when she managed her illness. Maybe he was too quick to write off her attempts at health because it hurt too much, the up and down of his mother's illness. But he was a big boy. He should have picked up the phone more, not dismissed Kayleigh when she talked about their mother, and answered the texts from his father.

In front of his parent's house, he stopped.

Same layout as Fiona's, the sunroom in the front, the kitchen in the back. But here was his mother's studio.

Two paintings stood propped up on easels, behind an overflowing desk and shelf that stored more paintings. His mother was frowning at one, with her hands on her hips, too focused on her work to notice him.

His dad came into the room, and his mother's face lit up, making her look younger. His dad put his arm around her waist, kissed her neck. His mother playfully swatted him away.

This was a rare sight. Usually, there was lots of yelling, his dad often storming out, then returning with a pile of groceries, then leaving again for a couple of days.

But he always came back, Quinn realized. He'd never abandoned him or his mother. Maybe his leaving for a few days was how he coped.

For whatever reason, Quinn had forgotten that, forgotten how much time his dad spent at Fiona's fixing the place. He didn't see until now how everyone made a hard situation work for the benefit of everyone because he had these people in his life who loved him.

And there was one person he wanted to share that with, his unconventional upbringing, his beautiful mother, his steadfast father, his energetic sister. He wanted to bring her here and show her where he had grown up, and, looking at his parents, Quinn realized he wanted what they had, a love that endured during their hardest hours.

His mother caught sight of him outside the window, and her face brightened. She waved at him to come in, smiling hugely.

Quinn raised a hand to them and ran up the three steps.

26

CHAPTER TWENTY-SIX

If only the circumstances weren't so awful, Simone would have enjoyed staying at the guesthouse that Marion had found for her in the suburbs.

It had a heated outdoor pool, a maze winding through a well-trimmed garden, and splendid views of the mountains. The soft colour palette made it a calm space, and with sleek contemporary furniture, it was the perfect place to stay for a weekend. But she missed her house, with her office, her garden, and all of her things, and not having a burnt-out hole in the front of it.

She couldn't believe it had happened, had spent every night since then, sleepless or waking up from fretful dreams.

Those dreams featured Quinn and seeing his expression as she called him a monster and told him to get away from her.

His enormous frame had tilted forward, and as Simone watched, the big Alpha man she knew looked small and shocked, his blue eyes almost turning black, the set of his jaw tight.

Quinn was the one to fulfil her fantasies, but she knew he didn't love her, that she had only been a mission to him, something his sense of duty felt compelled to take care of. She wished she hadn't said the "L" word to him. But it was true, and she couldn't tell herself it wasn't. She fingered the twisted gold strand of the necklace that had been delivered yesterday. The note has said simply: "This made me think of your hair, Quinn."

Quinn had been nothing but honest with her. He had his wounds, and he needed a woman who was content with playing.

Simone shifted on the couch, trying to concentrate on the file she was reviewing, specs on a house for a new client. She sighed and threw the file on the coffee table.

She couldn't get around the fact that he hadn't told her she was in danger. Her stomach dropped to the floor just thinking about it. He'd known since Meredith's wedding; he could have told her, but he'd decided she couldn't handle it. He had thought it would be better to lie to her. The only reason he was at Meredith's wedding was because JayJay had hired him. To murder her. It made Simone feel sick.

In the days following the explosion, Simone had hoped Meredith would visit, but she'd called. Her voice had been thick with sympathy. She said she was sorry, but she had to stick with her sister. Hearing the words had felt like being punched while she was down. Her best friend had tried to kill her, and her other best friend had abandoned her. Simone didn't think she could ever trust anyone again.

She shivered. She couldn't believe someone she had trusted for so long wanted to kill her. It was worse to go through this with her friends and without her lover.

Not her lover.

To go through this without the man she had the greatest sex of her life with. Simone snorted. Yeah, that was better.

The doorbell chimed, breaking the silence of the space.

Her heartbeat fluttered, and anticipation slid through her, a moment of hope rising to the top. Looking at the camera, her stomach rolled. She frowned at the black-and-white image that showed the front steps. It couldn't be.

Simone steeled herself as she opened the door. "Liam."

Her ex-husband stood there with his hands in his pockets. "Hello, Simone."

"Hi, there."

"I should have called first." Liam ran his hand over his head.

"Yes, a call would have been nice."

"I'm here now. Can I come in?"

She didn't want to let him in, but there was no one else right now, and she was lonely.

"Okay," she said and stepped back to let her ex-husband inside.

"I was in town to check on Mom, and I wanted to see you. It was awful. You two could have been seriously hurt or worse." Liam's hazel eyes watered.

"Yes, it was scary. But we're okay," Simone said.

Thanks to Quinn and his friend, they'd got out of there without a scratch.

"How have you been holding up?" Liam asked.

Simone stood behind the sofa, shaking her head. He'd up and left her, and now he cared about her?

"What do you want, Liam?"

"Do you need anything?" Liam stood in the doorway, twisting his hands.

"No. I'm okay," Simone said. She wasn't, but she would not share with the man who spent the last months of their marriage barely talking to her.

"It shook Mom," Liam said.

Thinking of Marion, Simone softened a bit. Liam had left his mother, just as he had left her.

"Yeah. She was over here last night, going through it all. I wish she had called the police when she found out that Carson, aka JayJay, had stolen all that money from her instead of just firing him. I would have helped her." Simone shook her head as a wave of sadness rolled over her. "Marion thinks JayJay trashed the house I was supposed to show in retaliation for being fired. I wish he'd stopped there." The bitterness in her voice took her back. But Marion didn't deserve her accounts being emptied, and she didn't deserve her house being destroyed. So yes, she was bitter. And looking at Liam, standing here, she tightened her hands into fists.

"She's a proud woman," Liam replied softly.

Yes, she was, and Simone knew under all that pride and bluster, was a woman with an enormous heart.

"I think she'll bounce back. She asked me if I would pose for a photo for her new campaign."

Liam's mouth twitched. He sat on the chair across from her. "Are you going to do it?"

Simone smiled. "I might. She's been good to me."

He looked at her with such a soulful expression, and that made her heart rate increase. He never showed her this much emotion when he was with her.

"Liam, what is it?"

"I just wanted to say... I'm sorry. I'm sorry for treating you so badly and for going through with the marriage. I didn't want to but felt I had to. I was in a job I didn't want, but I thought I had to keep it, and I was in a life I didn't want, but—"

"You never wanted me?" That shouldn't have hurt, but it did.

Shaking his head, Liam leaned over and took her hand in his.

"It's not like that. You are so kind and generous and beautiful. I was lucky you even looked at me. What I didn't want was all of this." Liam gestured around him. "This busy, all-consuming life. I didn't know how to express it then, and I'm sorry for all the hurt I caused you."

Simone pulled her hand out from under his. The old her would have told him it was okay. But now, the woman who'd had her feelings heard, her desires honoured? She didn't believe it was okay. She felt Liam was selfish and awful, and she didn't want to see him.

"Liam, get out," Simone said.

He put up his hands, gesturing for calm.

"Go, I don't want to talk to you. I'll always look after Marion, but right now, I can't see you. I blamed myself for you leaving me. It turns out you're just a selfish man who can't put anyone first because you find it too hard. Go."

"Simone, I thought maybe we could have dinner."

"Get out!"

She couldn't believe he thought she would just accept his apology. She didn't have to, and she would not blame herself for his immaturity. And she would not let herself hurt from it anymore, either.

"Okay, I'm going. Bye, Simone."

As soon as her ex-husband closed the door, Simone locked it.

She felt the tears well up, and she wiped her face. In her room, she huddled under the blankets, trying to clear her head.

There was one person she wanted to talk to about all of it, but she couldn't dial his number. Looking at the well-painted but blank walls, Simone picked up the business card with the infinity symbol on it, reached for her phone, and called someone about a painting.

27

CHAPTER TWENTY-SEVEN

As the big blond man beside her drummed his palm down on the steering wheel in tune with the bass, Simone wondered for the millionth time what she was doing here. Back in the borrowed bungalow, it had made perfect sense to find Quinn. Calling Xander under the pretense of buying paintings led to catching a ride on a private plane with Logan and some very serious-looking business people.

When they'd landed, Logan had collected a rented Range Rover then driven through the town.

"I need to see an old friend," he told her, parking the car in the driveway of a small house.

Following Logan up the driveway, around the house to the back, Simone saw a petite woman standing on a stool, taking things off a shelf over the sink. Logan rapped on the door, the woman startled, then her face broke out into a grin.

"Logan Marrock, get in here!" the women had cried. Logan grinned, threw his arms around the woman, nearly picking her up off the floor.

"Fiona, this is Simone. Simone, meet Fiona, a second mother to Quinn and good friend to me."

In the smallest kitchen Simone had ever seen, Fiona made them comfortable. She and Logan reminisced about when Quinn, Jordan, and Logan were in high school and then segued into tales of them coming home on leave. Seeing Fiona tear up, Simone squeezed her hand gently.

An hour later, there was another knock on the door, and a woman with long wavy hair and Quinn's blue eyes came in.

"Hello," she said, her gaze lighting on Simone. "I'm Deirdre." Her voice was soft and warm.

"This is Quinn's girl, Deirdre," Logan said.

Warmth flooded Simone's cheeks, but Deirdre's face broke out into a smile.

Fiona and Deirdre gushed over Simone while Logan sat back with a satisfied grin

A few hours later, as they approached the fishing cabin, Simone's stomach felt knotted. She wasn't sure this was a good idea. "Why are you taking me to him?"

Logan raised an eyebrow at her. "I thought that was what you wanted."

"Yes, I mean, I want to see him. I want to know why you're helping, why you brought me over to his mom's," Simone said.

Laughing, Logan reached over and squeezed her thigh. "We're brothers. It's how we roll. Quinn always had a hard time bringing people home to meet his mother. I thought I would break the ice."

"Because of Deirdre's mental health?"

Letting out a whistle, Logan nodded. "He's told you that. He must be in pretty deep. Yes, because his warm, caring mother, the woman who welcomed us all at her table, the one who has won national awards for her art, has bipolar disorder."

Swallowing a lump in her throat, Simone fidgeted with the strap of her bag. "I got the impression he doesn't want to bring people home because of that."

"Yes... and explaining how Fiona is like a mom to him. Personally, when I moved here, I thought Quinn was lucky, having a family. He has this quiet charisma that makes you want to be around him, you know."

Simone nodded. She envied Quinn for the number of people he had in his life. "I know."

"There were intense times when Quinn was growing up, but Deirdre has been stable for a while now. It's almost like he won't believe it because he's stuck in the past."

"The past is familiar and known," Simone said.

Her heart ached for Quinn, carrying around the pain of his mother's illness. Letting no one in because he didn't think anyone could accept his family.

"That it is, doll," Logan said.

"Will he be mad I'm coming?"

"We've seen how much he cares about you. When you called Xander, that was a green light to run interference." He shrugged. "I'm just the escort. The rest is up to the two of you."

Fat drops of rain splattered across the windshield. Simone tried to relax and settle back. This might not be a good idea. If he wanted her, he would have shown up at her door, Simone scoffed at herself. She had called him a monster and told him to get away from her. Quinn had respected her wishes. He'd also sent her the necklace. She fingered the strands at her throat and flushed. She should have trusted herself that what was between them was real and steady. If only she had gone away with him when he had asked her to. But then, what would have happened to Marion?

She needed to stop overthinking. He had left her that night at Club Bandit, but he'd come back. That was what mattered.

Instead of sending Quinn away, she should have asked him to be by her side. The last few weeks had been so stressful. He would have helped her carry that load, and he would have kept her distracted in all the best ways. Simone smiled, tracing a raindrop on the window. He had brought her out of her shell.

She understood Quinn not letting anyone become close to him. She had kept herself walled off from people because her father had taught her to hide her true feelings and expected her to do "the right thing." In her case, the right thing led to an unhappy marriage. When Liam had rejected her by dismissing her interest in kink, it had made her afraid of her wants.

Quinn made her voice her feelings, ask for what she wanted, and explore her desires.

He'd demanded everything from her in the bedroom, but it was always with her full consent, and every time she asked him to back off, he did. The man had walked through fire for her; he deserved better than being pushed away. Yes, he could have told her about the threat to her safety, but he did what he thought was best, and maybe she would have been able to handle it, but Simone could see how that might have posed a greater risk.

"You okay?" Logan asked. "You're quiet."

"Yeah, I'm fine." She sighed.

The canopy of trees split to reveal a clearing. "Good, because we're here."

As the SUV rolled over gravel, Simone grabbed onto the handlebar. Logan braked to a stop in front of a tiny wooden cabin.

Unclipping her seatbelt, Simone smoothed down her hair. Her palms were sweaty, and her heart was beating so fast she swore Logan could hear it by how he tilted his head and raised his eyebrow.

"You sure you're ready?"

Looking out at the choppy lake, Simone shook her head. But she needed to do this. "Does he know I'm coming?"

"What would be the fun of that?" Logan winked at her.

He was so infectious it was impossible not to like him. Simone gave him a small smile.

If Quinn didn't want to see her, she could always get a flight back home.

He had been honest with her the entire time. Even though he'd omitted the part about someone trying to set her on fire, Simone saw now how he had been trying to protect her, and that was something no one else had ever done for her.

Ever since her father had passed and even while married to Liam, she had been on her own.

She wasn't much better at this relationship stuff.

Staying behind Logan, Simone fidgeted with the strap on her bag, trying to swallow past the lump in her throat.

"Here we go," Logan said. He rapped once, twice on the door and stood back.

The door opened, glacier blue eyes met her, piercing right through to her core, and she looked down quickly and stepped aside as Quinn opened the door.

"Hey."

"Hi."

She studied Quinn's stocking feet. His socks were black with no holes, and they weren't stretched out of shape.

"Simone." Hearing Quinn say her name made her insides go liquid.

"Yes?"

She had almost forgotten how his brooding aura took up all the space. His muscles bulged under his black shirt, and his stare didn't leave her face.

As he took a step in her direction, her heart jumped. His rough hand on her cheek quelled her anxiousness, and she wanted to close her eyes and nuzzle into his touch.

"Want to come and see my man cave?" Quinn asked.

His smile made her relax a smidgen, and she brushed by him into the tiny cabin.

"Thanks, man," he murmured to Logan

"Anything for a Bandit Brother," said the other man. "You two have fun. Do all the things I would do. Bye, Simone." He tossed her a wave as he stepped away from the door.

"Bye," Simone said, giving him a wave in return.

Standing in the small space, Simone smiled. This was exactly what she'd thought Quinn's fishing cabin would be. Clean, functional, and the bare minimum.

"It's cute."

From his position against the door, Quinn raised an eyebrow. "Cute? You're calling my fishing cabin 'cute'?"

"Oh, it's very manly." She wondered if he could hear her thumping heart.

His long legs took three steps. Then he was in her space.

"What's with the fish?" Simone pointed to a brushed silver fish affixed to a plaque.

As Quinn took her hand in his, her cheeks grew warm.

"Jordan gave me that plaque as a gag gift. He said it was the only fish I was going to keep." A small smile played about his lips.

She loved how loyal she was to his friends, and her heart ached for his loss.

"I'm so sorry you lost him."

"Yeah, he was the best. Being here always brings back memories of him."

"I ambushed you. I could go back to town."

"No, it's perfect you are here. It's time to make fresh memories."

His words made her melt. She wanted to be with him. If it was in this much-loved fishing cabin or a penthouse apartment overlooking the Rockies, she didn't care, as long as he was in her view.

"You know, I would add some curtains," she mused aloud. "And a two-seater couch in front of the fireplace would be cozy."

She could see it in her mind, a rug on the worn floors, her snuggling with Quinn on the love seat in front of a crackling fire.

"You would make it unmanly." He put a finger under her chin, and her pulse raced. "Is that why you came? To redecorate my cabin?" Those piercing blue eyes wouldn't let her wiggle out of this one.

Looking away from him, Simone tried to calm her racing pulse. "I needed to come and see you, to tell you—"

"To tell me what?"

His eyes never left her face, and Simone bit her lip under his scrutiny. She couldn't get the words past the lump in her throat.

He reached with a thumb, ran it over lips. His fiery touch sent a shudder through her body.

"I'll always listen to you, baby."

"I wanted..." Simone swallowed hard. What if she said these words and he told her to go away?

"You can tell me."

Taking a deep breath, Simone leaned forward, her forehead touching his chest.

"To tell you, I'm so sorry for telling you to go away. I wish you had stayed with me that night."

She kept her head buried against the smooth plane of his chest. When his arms came around her, squeezing her tight, she let go of the breath she was holding.

"You had just found out one of your best friends betrayed you and watched your house explode," Quinn said. A muscle worked in his jaw. "I should have told you from the start that you were in danger."

His words eased the tension in her body. Relief washed over her. As his lips touched hers tenderly, Simone felt her body turn to liquid, the anxiety evaporating. His hand cupped the back of her neck. This was where she had wanted to be, in his arms.

Quinn broke off the kiss, framing her face in both his hands. He looked right into her eyes.

"I'm sorry I left you. I should have stayed by your side. Leaving when things get too tense is an unpleasant habit that I'm done with. I got into the habit of leaving because I didn't want to see if things turned out wrong. I'll never leave you again." Quinn kissed her, capturing her mouth with his.

As his tongue circled hers, Simone wrapped her hands around his waist. Quinn held her in place, his teeth nipping her lip slightly. This kiss felt like a promise. If that was a promise of his words or of things to come, Simone didn't know. She didn't care. She wanted him. Her arms came around his neck, hugging him to her. She didn't want to let him go.

Without breaking the kiss, Quinn slid her bag and coat off her shoulders, resting his hands on her waist. He lifted her, his hands cupping her ass.

A wave of desire rolled through Simone. She wanted him in her. Reaching up, she ran her fingers through his dark hair, put her hands on the back of his neck, pressing herself into him as close as she could.

She felt the low vibration from his chest as Quinn laughed.

"Feeling feisty?"

"I need you."

"I like the sound of that." He nuzzled her ear, nipped at her, and squeezed her butt cheeks, making Simone yelp. "Want to see my bed?"

"Yes," Simone said, feeling flushed at his intense gaze.

His tongue slipped into her mouth, demanding her compliance.

Her tongue danced with his, and she didn't know when she had experienced a better moment. All the moments with him were better.

Quinn set her down gently on the stairs, brushing his fingers through her hair.

"I love you," she said, the words escaping her lips again.

No... She closed her eyes, wanting to disappear. It was a perfect moment, and she'd ruined it once again.

"Simone." His deep tone compelled her to look at him.

"I'm sorry. I shouldn't have said that."

Quinn raised an eyebrow. "Is it untrue?"

Heat rose up her neck and into her face, but she shook her head. "No, it's true." The fluttering butterflies returned, the lump in her throat suddenly there again.

Quinn's gaze bore into her with such intensity. she might as well have been standing naked under a bright white light.

"I can go now," she whispered.

Taking her hand, Quinn pulled her close to his chest; his heartbeat thumped steadily under her cheek.

"There is nowhere for you to go because I'm right here." He took a step toward her, pushing her into the narrow staircase.

"I know, but I said those words again."

"Yes, you did. I want you to tell me everything, Simone. I want to know what you are feeling and thinking, and I like hearing those words from you."

His mouth consumed hers, kissing her as if he couldn't stop, wouldn't stop. She shivered as his hands ran over her waist, along her back. He broke the kiss, leaned down and touched her forehead with his.

"Get upstairs, woman," Quinn said.

With her heart thundering against her ribs, she climbed the last four steps to the loft space. She abruptly halted, her eyes widening at the sight of the king-sized bed that took up most of the loft.

"This is a gigantic bed in a small space."

The bed was flush to the left wall, with windows on the right side, which must flood this room with a light on a summer's day.

"I built it piece by piece."

"Don't you hit your head here on this low ceiling?"

"Every time." Quinn smiled.

He sat down on the edge of the bed, threading his fingers through hers, bringing her in between his legs. "Where were we?" he murmured as he wrapped his powerful arms around her.

"I don't know," Simone said.

"I wanted to show you my bed."

"It's a very nice bed."

He lifted her on his lap, and as his warmth engulfed her, her nipples beaded.

"It is a nice bed. We were at the part where I tell you I love you."

His words stunned her, made her catch her breath in her throat.

"Are—are you sure?" she stammered.

Quinn laughed. "Completely. I love you, Simone Roberts." He leaned into her. Then his velvet lips were on hers, his hands running up and down her back.

Her skin heated, she smiled, pushing at his muscled chest, trying to topple him onto the bed.

Quinn laughed, tugged her into his embrace, and fell onto the mattress.

Straddling his hips, Simone pushed her hair out of her face. She needed him in her now. "Fuck me hard."

28

CHAPTER TWENTY-EIGHT

As those words left her luscious lips, his entire body vibrated with an urgent need to ravage her from her pouty mouth to her pinkie toe. He brushed her hair from her face and stared into those teddy bear brown eyes.

He never could have imagined those words coming from the woman he first met at that wedding, that woman who blushed at everything and did her best to hide. Now here she was before him, confident and owning her sexuality, voicing her desires. With pride swelling in his chest, he kissed her lips until they were plump and red. He breathed in her tangy scent of arousal, amazed that his little bird was here with him.

"You have no idea how hard I'm going to fuck you." His hands trailed down her back, over her ass. He couldn't stop touching her. "I thought I lost you."

"I'm happy you let me in. I thought you would have closed the door on me."

"No. How could I?"

He sighed at her touch as her fingers slid under his shirt. Leaning forward, he pulled off her white blouse, kissing her collarbone. Her pulse jumped as his lips feathered her smooth skin.

"I will always let you in," he promised.

Undoing the clasp of her bra, he freed her perfectly round breasts. He brushed his thumbs over her nipples. Quinn locked eyes with her. "You asked. I'll deliver."

He sucked a nipple in his mouth, rolling his tongue over and around it. She whimpered above him, her hands on his shoulders. He scraped her nipple with his teeth, and her hips bucked against him.

"Easy there," he said, switching his attention to the other nipple. "You may be on top, but I'm still in charge."

Her head fell back, and her eyes closed, and she moaned. "More."

Taking his mouth off her other nipple, he pinched it hard.

"Open your eyes, Simone. I need to see you."

"Yes, Quinn." Her throaty purr sent all the blood to his cock.

Her hands pushed down on his shoulders, driving him back to her nipple. The taste of her flooded his brain, and his cock hardened into steel.

He tilted her back, his hands going to the waistband of her skirt. Slowly, he peeled the fabric down to her thigh, then lifted her leg over his and watched her shimmy out of the silky fabric.

"Want me to take this off?" she asked, her voice thick with desire, her hands hovering over the waistband of a rose-coloured thong.

"Yes. I want you naked all the time."

He picked her up, set her on the floor, and stood beside her, dropping his jeans and kicking them off.

"That's going to make it very hard to work." Simone giggled.

"Then don't."

She frowned, her mouth making a perfect pout.

"I was kidding," Quinn said with a chuckle. He pulled her close, kissing her shoulder, the hollow of her throat, wanting to erase that look of worry that had darkened her eyes.

"I know," Simone said, her hands coming around his shoulders. "I don't know what to do for work. I don't want to do the show anymore."

"We'll figure it out." He brushed her silky hair off her shoulders, traced a finger along her jawline. "My girl is smart."

"I just—" Simone bit her lip. She looked like she was going to cry, and it twisted Quinn's gut.

"Get on your knees, baby."

Her eyes grew wide at the dominance in his tone, and for a moment he wondered what she would do.

Without hesitation, Simone slid to her knees, looking at the floor.

He didn't think he had ever seen a woman so open and submissive, and he'd only given her the smallest taste of D/s.

He couldn't wait to explore with her and take her down that path after all.

"Come right here," he said, guiding her so that her cheek was resting on his thigh.

"Tell me what's upsetting you. I'm all the way in, Simone. I want to know every worry, every bad dream, every red light you get."

He stroked her hair, sensed her breathing calm.

"I'm sorry I killed our mood."

"You did nothing to our mood. If you reach your hand over a few inches, you'll find that I'm still in the mood."

Tentatively, she glided her hand over to his cock, and her touch sent a blaze of need through his body.

"I see." The smile in her voice made him grin in answer.

"Tell me what's on your mind."

"Before everything that happened, I loved being on the show. I enjoyed showing people straightforward ways to make a space beautiful. But I don't want to do it anymore. I feel as if I have to keep that job because Marion getting it for me caused so much damage."

Quinn stroked her hair. He knew what it was like to feel guilty for another person's action, and he would not let Simone take that on.

"That's not on you, Simone. You didn't throw the explosives into your own house. You simply took a job that was offered to you. Accepting or keeping a job doesn't justify what they did."

"Despite that, maybe Ava was in pain, and I didn't see it. I feel like I need to keep the job because other people were in that contest."

"And they didn't destroy your house, Simone. They went on with their lives. You're a great friend. Ava is a horrible person."

Her peal of laughter soothed the tight knot in his gut. He wrapped his hand around her hair, tugging her gently.

Those big brown eyes stared at him as she slid her hands around his leg, moving between his feet. Taking his cock in her hand, she put her pink lips around it and sucked.

"Oh, that's a good girl," he hissed as she swallowed on his cock.

With a hand on her hair, he pulled and felt the vibration of her moan around his sensitive skin. She licked the underside of his head and back down the length. Quinn knew in another moment he would let go, and she would suck him dry. As wonderful as that thought was, he wanted to be buried in her pussy. Tugging on her hair, Quinn nearly changed his mind at the look of disappointment she gave him.

"I want you on the bed, spread wide for me."

"Yes, Quinn."

Her agreement rushed more blood to his cock, and he helped her onto the mattress.

Standing at the end of the bed, noticing her hair fan out behind her, her widely spread legs inviting him in, Quinn shook his head. "Gorgeous. I told you that, yes?"

"You did."

"I'm going to tell you every day." He got on the bed, his hands holding her legs open, kissing every inch of her legs from her ankles to her thighs.

"Then I'll start believing it."

"Damn right you will. I've missed this pussy." He breathed in her scent and knew he could stay buried in her folds forever. He leaned in, gliding his tongue over and around her clit. Simone moaned, and he laughed. "I'm going to unravel you."

Plunging into her soft depths with both his finger and tongue, Quinn licked and lapped, feeling her muscles contract for him, hearing her sounds of pleasure. Sucking on her pebbled nub, he swirled his tongue around the hot centre, then pulled out. Moving over her body, pressing his chest to hers. With a hand on either side of her shoulders, Quinn hovered inches above her face. She was clutching the bedsheets, a fine sheen of sweat on her brow and a little pout on that precious mouth.

"I want you. Just you, with nothing between us. How do you feel about that?"

"Yes, I want that too."

"Marry me, Simone Roberts." He kissed her mouth.

She mewled, arching into him, and her arms came around his neck. "Okay," she said when Quinn came up for air.

"Okay?" He knew he was grinning like a cartoon character.

"Yes, I'll marry you."

A weight lifted off his shoulders. His heart knew she was his long before his head caught up.

Sliding down her body, he trailed a path of light kisses on her silky skin, pausing at her entrance. He looked at her, laid out on his bed in his cabin, and knew he was one lucky bastard.

"I'll make you the happiest woman ever," he promised.

"I'm waiting." Simone smiled.

The first thrust felt like nirvana, her velvety skin around his shaft.

"More."

With one more thrust, he was balls deep in her pussy, her tightness closing around him. "Play with your nipples," he ordered.

For a moment, Simone hesitated, and he withdrew from her.

"Yes, Quinn," she said.

He watched as she took a nipple in between her thumb and index finger and twisted it. "Harder."

He waited until she winced and slid back into her, thrusting deep. Teaching his little bird about D/s was going to be a fun challenge.

He took her leg and brought it over her shoulder, and Simone cried out at the deeper angle. He pulled back her hood with his thumb and finger and rubbed her clit as he thrust, long and deep.

Simone cried out, arching to meet his thrusts. He wanted to speed this up, to find the promise of sweet release, but he also wanted to slow it down, to have it etched into his memory how perfect she looked.

But he would have every day to look at her, every day to tease out more of her desires and to try them on, every day to bring her to bliss, over and over again.

He probably didn't deserve her, but he was going to make sure she never regretted saying yes to him.

The feel of her swollen pussy was like coming home.

His tongue plunged into her mouth in time with his cock, and she arched under him.

"Come with me, baby," Quinn said.

Her arms came around his neck, her moans urging him on. The flame of desire down his back was too large to ignore.

"Quinn!" Her nails dug into his shoulders.

He welcomed the bit of pain as she contracted hard around him; he let go, his hot seed releasing into her core, and he shuddered.

He laughed, shifted his weight, so he didn't crush her, and settled her head on his chest, wrapping an arm around her.

"What did you think about that, wife?"

Her bright smile made his heart gush.

"I think I'm going to need to do more Pilates."

"I'll build you an in-home studio, where you can do Pilates naked."

"Just what a girl wants," she said. A look of concern darkened her expression.

Kissing her furrowed brow, Quinn snuggled her closer on his shoulder. "You're thinking again. What is it?"

"Where are we going to live?"

"Together."

"When are we going to get married?"

"As soon as possible."

Grinning at him, Simone reached beside her and threw a pillow at him. "I'm serious."

He kissed the back of her neck and rubbed her back. "Baby, wherever you want to live, that's fine with me, and I'm seriously going to put a ring on your finger as soon as possible."

Moving down, so she was on his chest, she buried her mouth against his chest. "Or a collar on my neck," she whispered.

Quinn's breath stilled, his hand threaded through her hair. Gently, he cupped her chin. "Is that what you want?" he asked. With his heart pounding in his chest, he was afraid to hear the answer.

"Yes, Quinn."

Leaning down to meet her lips, Quinn kissed her softly.

"Tell me why."

"I had a conventional marriage. It didn't work. I know that's because my ex wasn't in it, but I was in it for the wrong reasons, too. I'm committing to being your submissive. I'm committing because I love you. After all, I am safe with you because I feel strong with you, and I feel like I belong to you."

"We belong to each other." Choked up, he put an arm around his wife- and submissive-to-be and kissed her forehead.

"We are going to talk it out, Simone. I will not do this half-assed. I don't just want kink in the bedroom. I want D/s."

She stilled in his arms, and for a moment, he thought he had scared her.

"You fulfilled my fantasies and made me feel brave. I want something I can give myself to, too." She nodded. "I'm in, Quinn. A beautiful necklace showed up at my door," Simone grinned at him.

He couldn't speak past the lump in his throat, so he crashed into her sweet lips, kissing her with all the ownership he felt.

29

CHAPTER TWENTY-NINE

As the cool breeze came off the lake, Simone leaned against Quinn's chest for warmth. The new moon glowed in the sky overhead, and Simone could envision how pretty this place was in the summer.

"Perfect place for a wedding, don't you think?" Quinn said in her ear.

"I think it would be hard to get people here, and there's only one bed."

"People can deal with it," Quinn said.

Simone laughed and playfully swatted his arm.

"And what about the one bed?"

"Minor detail."

The enormous bed was comfortable, and for the last two days, they had only left it for essentials.

"Hey!" Logan came up the path with a pizza box in hand.

Simone squirmed on Quinn's lap.

"Stay right here."

It made her blush, thinking of this afternoon's romp in that bed, and she knew the cabin walls were thin, and Logan had probably heard her.

"I'll rent out the whole lake."

"I don't care. You can plan it all."

She meant it too. Her first attempt at marriage hadn't ended well, and she had pored over every single detail. This time, she wanted it to be different.

"We need an event planner. Is that from Martha's?"

Logan put the pizza box on the table and pulled up a chair. "You know it. With my mom moving down to Toronto, this is the only reason I have to come back."

Logan opened the box, put a slice on a paper plate, and handed it to her.

With the two men watching, Simone took a bite.

"That's good," she said around a mouthful.

"It's the best. I missed it so much."

"You don't visit enough." Logan reached over and grabbed a slice of pizza.

"Speaking of that, I have to take Simone by to meet the folks."

Logan hadn't told him? Then Simone realized she hadn't told him either. She started coughing frantically.

"Already done, man," Logan said with a grin. "Except for your dad. He was out on a job. We made a stop on the way up."

Watching Quinn's face, Simone breathed a sigh of relief. He didn't look mad.

"I'm sorry I didn't tell you."

"Why didn't you?" Quinn asked.

Fidgeting slightly under his intense gaze, Simone shrugged.

"It wasn't a big deal. I met Fiona and your mom. They were both nice. We've been busy."

Logan laughed and clapped Quinn on the back. "She's right."

Simone knew her cheeks were flaming, and she hid her face against Quinn's chest.

"I guess that's one less thing off the list," Quinn said, squeezing her hand. "But you got to tell me everything, Simone."

"Yes, Quinn." She offered a smile. "Deirdre wasn't what I expected," she said, trying to take the two men's focus off her squirming.

"Deirdre's great," Logan cut in. "Who wouldn't want her for a mom?"

As Quinn turned his gaze on Logan, the big blond man raised his arms. "Hey man, I'm not saying it was easy. I'm just saying you could have done worse."

"You're right. If I gave you the impression that she was cold, that was my fault. I'm the one who detached. I think that's how I coped with her illness, by convincing myself that she didn't care or she was horrible. But she cared a lot, and she isn't a horrible person."

"Her illness affected you a great deal," allowed Simone. "It makes sense you had a coping mechanism. She and Fiona both gushed over me and made me feel cared for."

"Good."

As he rubbed his thumb on her lip, Simone developed an ache between her legs and found herself growing wet. This man had woken up her sexuality, and there was no going back.

Quinn leaned forward and kissed her.

Simone closed her eyes, getting lost in the sensation of his tongue encircling hers.

"Maybe my mom knows an event planner."

"You need an event planner for what?" Logan prompted finally.

If the big grin on his face was anything to go by, Simone had a hunch their friend had guessed.

"She's agreed to marry me."

Sliding off his lap, Simone grinned in response to Logan's infectious grin.

"Yes!" Logan got up, rattling the table, and punched his fist in the air. "That's outstanding, man!"

As the two men embraced, Simone knew she was going to have a huge influx of alpha males in her life, and she couldn't wait.

"I have the perfect person in mind," Logan said. He took out his cell.

She wondered what Marion would think, though Simone knew her former mother-in-law would be genuinely happy for them.

"Hey, Harper, how's it going?"

Quinn raised his eyebrows and started shaking his head. Logan made a shooing gesture with his hand.

"Yeah, that's tough," he said. "Are you still looking to plan events on the side? I have friends who need help with a wedding."

Slightly fascinated, Simone watched Quinn's expression darken.

"Quinn is going to marry Simone, the designer chick from the morning show," Logan said. His clear delight widened his grin. "I know, wild, right? I'll text you her details. Thanks, Harper, you're the best."

Quinn let out a low whistle and shook his head. "You can't touch her, man."

"Who said anything about touching her? She's a friend and good at what she does," Logan said.

"She's under Xander's protection."

"That doesn't mean I can't be friends with her," Logan said.

But from the way Logan crossed his arms over his chest, Quinn had hit a nerve.

"Why does she need protecting?" Simone asked.

As the two men exchanged raised eyebrows, Simone looked at the ground.

"She needs training," Logan said.

"I got it."

Simone smiled at the growl in Quinn's voice.

"A protector is an experienced Dom who looks out for an inexperienced sub. Maybe that person is new to playing or is unattached and doesn't want attention or doesn't want to say no or engage."

Simone couldn't imagine being single and going to a BDSM club, so it made sense.

"If I want to play with Harper, I'll have to ask Xander first," Logan explained.

"And he doesn't like to share," added Quinn.

Leaning back in the chair, Simone shook her head. There was so much about his world that she didn't understand.

"He's her employer, nothing more," Logan said, his face a mask of stone.

Quinn put his hands up in a gesture of peace then wrapped one around her neck and kissed her where it met her shoulder. "I'm taking you to Club Bandit as soon as we get home."

"I can't wait," Simone said. She wanted to be flogged again, she wanted to try the other stuff she had seen in Quinn's bag too.

"Have you guys decided where you are going to live?" Logan asked.

They had talked about it all last night, in between him making her scream over and over. They had planned out where they were going to live and what they were going to do.

"We're going to buy the bungalow I've been staying in from Marion," Simone said.

"I'm going to stay working for Axis Management for now," Quinn said.

Logan's eyes widened. "You sure?"

"I want to see if I can put the past behind me. Plus, Kayleigh is out there, and I want to be close to her."

Simone felt like her heart was going to burst. She loved Quinn's loyalty and his protectiveness, and she felt so lucky that this man loved her.

Quinn reached for her hand. His was so big and strong, hers swam in it, and it felt so right.

"We haven't figured out all the wedding details yet, but there is one thing I know. Will you be my best man?"

Simone caught the tiny tear forming in Logan's eye before he ducked it away. He reached out his arm and clasped Quinn's.

"I'll make Jordan proud," he said.

Shaking his head, he returned his clasp.

"I wish he was here, and if he was, it would be both you and him. The two of you have always had my back. You're not a replacement for him, Logan."

"There is no replacement for that guy," Logan said.

"No," Quinn said.

"We were going to remember him, a memorial just for us, that's what we said, right? Do you think you're ready?"

Holding up their clasped hands, Quinn nodded.

"I'm ready," he said. "What about you?"

As he looked at her, with that intense blue stare, Simone knew whatever came at them, they would solve it together. Her heart ached for him, for his loss and his pain, but she hoped she could shoulder that with him.

"Can't wait," she said.

As Quinn put his hand on the back of her neck and kissed her deeply, she knew they were ready for anything.

The End

30

ACKNOWLEDGEMEN

Thank you to my mate and my cubs for giving me the bits of time and space to wrangle the words. Thanks to my dearest; just add it to my tab.

For their friendship, support and many takes of beta reading, thank you to the Crit Chicks and Author K.S. Ellis; y'all make this writing thing a ton easier.

Thank-you for Amy, for being the first person to tell me, "I LOVE it."

Thanks to Jess and Olivia for reading an early draft; your enthusiasm was the momentum I needed to get to the end.

Thank you to Tiffany for the cover and for bringing me into this decade of publishing.

Special thanks to authors Ivy Whitaker and Jenni Bara, who made this book better.

CONNECT WITH RALEIGH

I love hearing from readers! If you want to know when my upcoming release is, check out my website: https://raleighdamson.com

If you enjoyed Flame For You, please consider leaving a review!

You can find me on Twitter: @DamsonSnow and on Instagram: @RaleighDamsonBooks

You can sign-up for my weekly newsletter, where I share book things and point at things, here.

The next book in the Bandit Brothers series is FLAME FOR TWO and you can pre-order, here: https://books2read.com/u/mZZ082

FLAME FOR TWO BY RALEIGH DAMSON

He can have anything in the world, except her

Xander Montague: billionaire and genius, co-CEO of Axis Management.

He saved Harper Blake from her crime family's snare.

He wants nothing more than to completely possess her, but after destroying his last submissive, the most he can give is his protection.

All on the line

Logan Marrock: Private operative, adrenaline junkie, rope expert: never met a risk he won't take. From the moment he saw Harper, he wanted her, determined to get past her walls.

He can give Harper what she craves.

She's worth the risk of Xander's wrath.

No more secrets

Harper wants Xander to see her as the woman she's become, not the scared girl he rescued.

As his executive assistant, she keeps Xander's secrets but is done hiding her own. The more Xander pushes her away, the more Harper turns to Logan.

The past isn't done

And Xander realizes Logan is perfect for her.

Logan sees the bond between them and it makes him question everything he feels.

Not all risks pay off

When trouble finds Logan, Xander comes to his aid and they start to see what Harper has known all along: she can flame for two.